A FRIENDLY LITTLE MURDER

A VIOLET CARLYLE HISTORICAL MYSTERY

BETH BYERS

SUMMARY

August 1925

After a slew of cases for Jack, a new book, and a series of business meetings for Vi, and an excess of Violet's step-mother for them both, Vi and Jack determine to flee to a lodge in the woods. A little fresh air, a ramble or two, afternoon naps, lingering mornings over a cup of Turkish coffee and perhaps all will be aright again.

Only one morning walk ends with a body and yet again, Violet, Jack, and their friends find themselves involved in a mysterious death. The main suspects for the killer are none other than the victim's long-time friends. Just why do you turn on an old friend? And if you've done it once, will you do it again?

CHAPTER 1

The train was lumbering along as though the engine was too hot to continue. It sputtered and moaned. With the heat of the day, the press of the bodies, and the general closeness of the carriage, Violet felt certain she might die a slow and terrible death on this *very* train journey.

"Was this a good idea?" Lila moaned. Her eyes were closed and she was waving a fan in front of her face. "None of us even hunt. Why are we doing what the earl does and going to a hunting lodge? Even if it's more a hotel pretending to be a hunting lodge. Violet, does your father seem like a happy man to you?"

Before Violet could answer, Lila continued, "Violet and Jack should have bought a yacht, and we should be somewhere in the sea with an ocean breeze."

"Don't say such things," Violet said, waving her own fan more fervently. "It just makes this train more stifling."

"The earl seems to enjoy going away on his trips," Jack

said calmly. Despite the sweat at the edge of his face and the fact that he'd abandoned his coat and rolled up his sleeves, he seemed impervious to the heat.

"He doesn't enjoy going on trips," Denny groaned, mopping his face and grumbling. "He enjoys leaving his wife for an extended period."

Vi would have laughed but it was too hot to laugh. She took in a deep breath and then blew out the air to fan over her face, but her own warm breath wasn't helping with the heat.

"If this train weren't going so very slow," Ham said, "we'd have the cross-breeze to blow that woman's perfume the other way. She's poisoned the air."

Violet glanced towards the woman sitting with her companions. Her gaze was followed by the entirety of their group.

"Anyone else feel like they're looking in a mirror?" Denny asked casually. Both groups contained two couples and an extraneous friend. The other group, however, had an extra female rather than an extra male.

Regardless, both had a man in a tan jacket—Denny on their side—and a man in a dark blue jacket with pin-gray stripes—this was Jack, though his jacket was laid over the back of the seat behind them. Violet and a blonde across the way were both wearing nude pink dresses, gray cloches, and sensible brown shoes for traveling. Given the heat, every female had a fan in her hand. Lila and the second woman both wore loose pink dresses and to Violet's surprise, the other woman was clearly expecting. Lila, however, was as slim as ever.

The pregnant woman was the one wearing too much perfume. She was also wearing a rather heavy layer of makeup. Violet wasn't one to judge the use of makeup, but in this circumstance, it wasn't the makeup that was bothering Violet. It was having an extra layer of *anything* in this heat.

If she weren't on a train, she'd have been in her underthings laying across her bed waiting for the heat of the day to pass or she'd be in an icy bath.

Vi glanced again at the others in the group. Any kind of distraction would do and with her next glance, Vi noted the fifth member of the other friend group. She was a woman with round spectacles and a wicked expression. She was glistening from the heat, but it didn't seem to stop her willingness to hellishly tease her friends. Violet recognized the expression. It was a classic Vi maneuver and engendered instant delight.

The woman had elfin features with dark hair that curled in spirals. Rather than fighting her hair, she seemed to embrace the curls, or perhaps she'd given up the fight. Her eyes were slanted just enough to make them particularly intriguing. She had a dimple in her chin and another in her cheek. She was, simply put, adorable.

Among Violet's friends, Hamilton was the fifth, and oldest, member. To Violet's shocked delight, both the extraneous woman and the extraneous Hamilton were wearing brown. Hamilton was wearing a brown jacket and pants with a rather nice mustard shirt that few could pull off well. The woman with the expression that declared she'd just said something naughty was wearing a pinstriped brown dress with a mustard sash about the waist.

"Poor Ham," Lila said. "You'll have to be our excess of female so we match properly."

Ham ran his hand over his close cropped beard. "I rather think that your Denny fills that role better than I."

Vi grinned and leaned into Jack's side. "You are the one in brown and yellow, my darling Hamilton."

He winked before he said dryly to Lila, "But yon Denny is the most feminine of this group, your sweet self and Violet included."

"Lila isn't sweet," Violet and Denny said in unison, with Denny adding, "She's a dangerous creature who took away my chocolate. She's mean and vicious, really. You should watch her. You never know when she'll turn on you."

"You're fat again," Lila told him without sympathy. "Of the two of us, the only one who gets to be too round to run is me and that has an end date, laddie. You might as well accept it that you'll have to move, sweat, and go without chocolate until you can fit into that grey suit I bought you."

"It was too small from the start," Denny whined.

"Have faith, my friend," Violet said. "You'll slim down just sitting on this train."

Violet let her head rest on Jack's shoulder and used the fan dramatically, including Jack in the wind. She and Jack were in full, unashamed retreat. Hunting lodge or no, they weren't rushing to the country to do anything more than escape Lady Eleanor's appearance at their door.

Retreat. Full retreat and nothing less. No other description would be accurate. They'd returned the young wart, Violet's brother Geoffrey, to Lady Eleanor and the earl. Geoffrey hadn't been changed so much as revealed himself as occasionally human. Even still, Lady Eleanor had turned on Violet—yet again—and she and Jack

4

decided to pull a page from the earl's book and flee to a hunting lodge.

"Do you intend to hunt?" Denny asked Jack. Denny pulled on his collar again as if yanking at it could lower the heat.

"I plan to walk about a bit with binoculars rather than a rifle. Not much of a man for shooting things down since the war." Jack's wide shoulders shifted and Violet wound her fingers through his. She didn't like to think of him in the war. Even if he wasn't in the trenches, he'd been recruited into the military police, and he suffered along with the other soldiers. He had been lucky in comparison, and he was quick to say it.

Jack was a large man. Not so much handsome in the traditional sense as solid and reliable. He made her feel delicate and beloved. There was something about his dark hair, dark eyes, and penetrating gaze that said he missed nothing of what was happening around them, but in particular, that he missed nothing about Violet.

"What about you, Ham?" Denny asked.

"I've been on case after case since—" He didn't finish the statement, but they could all finish it. He'd been on case after case since their friend, Rita, had left England for another foreign adventure. He cleared his throat. "I want nothing more than to smoke some cigars, drink a few Old Fashioneds and nap in an overstuffed chair. Napping in a bed is for old men. Real men put up their feet and pretend to be having deep thoughts. Perhaps pondering on some treatise or other."

Lila groaned, fanning herself, and Denny nodded in agreement with Hamilton. Lila was very pale while Denny was golden. She was lush and lovely and stylish, and

Denny was a blond, dapper fellow, although Violet felt certain that Denny's dapperness came from Lila's shopping. He had been at the plumper end of his range before Lila had stepped in. His theory that Lila had bought him a smaller-than-usual suit had been, in fact, Violet's idea. "I could get behind all that. But napping in a bed is also for married couples and children."

"I'd nap in a bed. It's my preferred spot," Violet said with a grin. "And I'll walk in the woods with you," Violet told Jack when she realized that neither of his friends wanted to go along.

"Ah," Denny teased, "young love."

"Not lazy love," Lila countered, poking him with her elbow. "Unlike you. You're a chubby duckling."

"Bright young healthy types," Denny added, shaking his head. "They'll learn."

Violet closed her eyes against their smirks and if Jack was amused, he didn't show it. Hamilton stretched as he said, "I could be persuaded for a swim. It's too hot to ramble unless it's very early, and I have every intention of sleeping in."

"Did you decide to add a swimming pool to the country house?" Denny asked idly. "We should be there, swimming. Since apparently you weren't excited about the idea of a yacht."

Violet shook her head and Jack answered, "We were distracted by break-ins, babies, and murders. Perhaps you recall?" He paused. "Did you get the letter from Gwen and John? They had a baby boy. There are small baskets with squalling creatures all about that people are thrilled have arrived."

"Ah," Denny said, "the mighty heir. We're having a girl."

Denny grinned confidently. "Any boy of mine will be a complete waste of time and energy. Girls, however, especially ones like Lila, they might have a chance. If the girl is like me, God help her." Denny looked as though he'd been struck by a brilliant thought and then shook it off. "How hard is it to choose a place for the swimming pool and tell your servants to arrange it?"

"Harder than you'd think," Jack replied dryly. "I don't believe we discussed it once or even thought about it."

"Please," Denny shot back. "Violet bought into a new chocolate business, she moved the woman and her family to Bath to set up shop in a bigger town and have a greater chance of success, she persuaded your cousins to help us find a killer, she saved Victor's babies from burglars, and she finished writing that book."

"We all know Vi is super human and cannot be compared to us lesser mortals." Jack shifted a little and she felt his arm wrap around her. It really was too hot for snuggling, even before adding in the close quarters of the train, but she didn't mind. It had been hard to relax for too long.

She glanced towards their counterparts across the aisle and saw the woman with the mischievous expression eyeing them rather interestedly. She was, Violet was reminded again, rather like herself. They both had sharp features and slim figures. Each of them carried a leather satchel and both had a book in their lap. Was the girl reading the new Edgar Rice Burroughs book as well, or could she be like Violet's sister-in-law and perusing some treatise or a series of essays? As much as Violet loved her twin's wife, she hoped the girl across the aisle was reading the *Princess of Mars.*

Lila rolled her eyes and lazily fanned herself. "I'd demand something with ice, but anything they brought onto the train holding the ice surely has melted by now."

"It does seem likely," Ham agreed. "This weather feels ridiculously unseasonable."

"It is August," Violet told him. "I believe it tends to be hotter during August."

"I'm a detective, you know," Ham said with an amused look. "I've figured that out."

"They'll get more ice at the next stop," Violet smirked, eyes still closed.

"As a detective," Ham interjected with a grin that only reached the corners of his mouth and was nearly as hard to see as one of Jack's, "all clues do point to us needing to go to the sea. Lila is right. You should have bought a yacht."

"I always am," Lila said without opening her eyes. She curled onto her side and tucked her head onto Denny's shoulder. She was right, Violet thought, and felt sleep beckoning to her as well. She was being smothered into it by the heat and by the sleeplessness of her last few weeks. She took a deep breath in as Jack trailed his finger down her arm. It was all she needed to finish her own journey to sleep.

CHAPTER 2

*T*he train chugged to a stop and Violet woke confused at the change of movement. She felt Jack's arm around her, but the usual comfort of it was different, and it took her far too long to realize she was leaning against him, sitting up. It was only then that she took in the murmur of voices. The smell of coal that reminded her of the train and where she was came back to her in a flood.

She kept herself still. It was so hot, if she pretended to be asleep, perhaps she'd be able to slip back into unconsciousness and miss the heat of the rest of this journey.

It took her long moments of half-asleep baking on the train to realize she was hearing more than just her friends. It took her so long to realize the group of look-a-likes had turned in their seats and were telling tales with Ham and Denny that Violet was worried about her reasoning.

Violet watched through her lashes for a few minutes. Denny was telling one of his tall, gossipy tales around a cigarette hanging from his mouth. As she snuck her extended peek, she noticed the other group's pregnant woman stand and cast a nasty glance at her husband that went unseen by the others.

The woman placed a hand on her stomach. "I do need to stretch my legs." There was such a telling command in her statement, but no one paid her any attention except the single woman among her friends, and the look she gave was pitying.

Violet would have expected one of the pregnant woman's party to go with her, and it seemed the other woman expected the same, but the only reply she got was a, "Enjoy yourself, Pamela m'dear." Her husband turned back to the other couple traveling with them and laughed at something the other married woman said. The three of them did look awfully chummy, the poor little kitten.

"Lyle!" Pregnant Pamela hissed, but he merely gave her a wink and turned back to the others. The look Pamela gave her husband was nothing short of a killing blow. Nearly as vicious was the look Pamela sent towards the others, but again, only the curly-haired woman who matched Ham noticed with the same pitying wince.

As the pregnant woman walked away in a cloud of perfume, Violet glanced towards Lila and saw her eyes were cracked as well. Their gazes met, and they smiled just enough to admit to the other that they were spying. Lila's narrowly opened gaze dropped just on the left side as she had a shadow of a giggle that caused Denny to glance her way, but he didn't react.

There was, however, little doubt in Violet's mind that both Denny and Jack were aware that they'd woken up. Violet suspected that the pregnant woman was particularly angry that her husband was oblivious to her scathing looks.

Violet decided that the time for feigning sleep was over.

"Here she is," Denny said as Violet sat up, blinking blearily, gaze following the pregnant woman who was stalking off. "The lady of the hour."

"What am I?" Lila asked as she put off her own pretense at sleeping. "Tinned sardines?"

Violet laughed and then faced the people who had joined her party. "Excuse me. I think I lost the battle against the heat. I'm Violet Wakefield."

The married woman from the other side of the aisle said, "You won it, I think. Sleeping against a lovely set of shoulders like your husband's and being unaware of this journey isn't losing, it's winning, darling."

Violet smiled automatically, but she felt as though the other woman—the married woman no less—had just sized up Jack and found him desirable. In fact, Violet realized, that *was* what just happened. What an odd feeling, Violet thought.

Her gaze flicked to Ham and saw that he had seen what she had, and he was amused in the extreme. The curly-haired woman with the wicked expression noted it as well and smirked nearly as broadly. Violet hid her annoyance. The woman was sitting *right* next to her husband. One would think she'd at least wait until her husband wasn't there.

Violet stretched to allow herself to unobtrusively see Jack's face. It was entirely impassive, which told Violet he'd felt weighed and noticed. She winked at him and then

turned back to the others. "I believe I slept through intro-
ductions."

"You were snoring quite delightfully," the young
woman said, her expression devilish but with an air of
friendliness about it.

"Vi is generally delightful, even snoring," Ham told the
woman. "Jovie, meet Violet Wakefield. Vi, this is Miss
Jovie Webb."

The bespectacled woman in brown and mustard
waved lightly.

Ham gestured to the oblivious husband. "This is Lyle
Craft. His wife, Pamela, just went for a walk."

The woman who had sized up Jack and found him
desirable was Fanny Browne, with her husband, Michael,
next to her. Violet nodded to them all and learned they
were all going to the same oversized blend of hunting
lodge and hotel.

It was in the Lake District near Scafell and was said to
have rather a lot of lovely outdoor activities. Jack had
been immediately intrigued while Violet didn't care as
long as it was far, far, far from Lady Eleanor. Vi's father
had suggested the luxury hunting lodge and Jack had
booked suites before the day had ended.

To be honest, Vi would just as soon have gone back to
the country house and loved on Victor's babies until they
were big enough to tell her to go away. Only Victor had
been ordered to bring the little twins and Kate to his
mother-in-law with the threat of dire consequences.

Violet was slow to recover from her nap, so she
listened to the chatter with little comment. Feeling rather
as though her head had been dipped in wool, she knew it

was the lack of sleep. Occasional cat naps with long nights of nightmares just wasn't enough.

Vi was being taken down by the dreams again. After the murder in the country house followed by a break-in where Victor's twin babies had been at risk, she hadn't slept well for weeks.

Vi was sure that Jack had dragged her to London to see if a change of scenery would help with Violet's sleep, and when it didn't, he was dragging her off again. She had little doubt he'd drag her around the countryside with the wholesome air and the beautiful sights until her body remembered how to sleep at night. Perhaps by then they could go back to the country house and be there when the babies returned.

The train ride finished before Violet could slide fully back into sleep, and she was encompassed with gathering her things and getting off the train. "I want a cool bath," Violet told Jack. "A nap, ginger wine, and something cold. Ice cream? Lemon ice? I'm not picky."

"You are too," Denny said. "She wants chocolate ice cream. Several scoops. Have it sent to my room, and I'll hand deliver to Violet, so she doesn't have to quibble with the servants."

"I could go for one of those as well," Jovie answered, winking at Denny. "Order one for me as well." She hooked her hand through Violet's. "Walk with me, would you?"

Violet blinked in surprise, but she followed Jovie off the train. As they stepped down into the station, each of them carrying a leather satchel that university students used, Jovie said, "Your friend Ham…"

Violet waited, already guessing where this was going.

"…he's a bachelor?"

Violet nodded.

"He's entirely unattached?"

That was the rub, wasn't it? Violet was rather sure that Hamilton was very much attached. The object of his affection, however, had fled the country after Ham had sidestepped her, given that Rita was ridiculously wealthy and he was a working inspector.

"It's complicated," Violet said with a shrug. "I can't give you the details, but he's not a safe bet."

Jovie nodded. She seemed to be seeing something that no one else could. Instead she added, "He's rather manly, isn't he? Like your Jack. They feel...dangerous...in my head."

Violet considered what Jovie was saying and found herself more baffled that this near stranger was speaking to her of Jack's attractions.

"All men are dangerous in my experience," Violet said quellingly. "Give them the right set of circumstances and any of us are quite dangerous. Women are much the same."

Jovie shrugged Violet's statement off. "There's just something about fellows like Jack and Ham. The rest of them feel like paper dolls. I enjoy a vital man." At Violet's expression, Jovie laughed and then patted her cheek lightly. "Don't worry. I heard your warning about Hamilton, and I'd never step into another woman's place. I'm sure my mother would prefer I was not many things I am, but of that sin, she can feel assured."

Violet didn't have a reply other than a sarcastic snort, which she held back. If she'd have known Jovie better, Vi wouldn't have bothered to hold back. Instead she looked about for the objects of their conversation and found them standing with Jovie's friends near a uniformed man. Jack waved her over and Violet told Jovie, "We're being beckoned."

Violet started towards her friends but turned back when Jovie didn't. Taking in Jovie's expression, Vi said honestly, "Ham is taken in all the ways that matter, as far as I can tell."

"I'm guessing what you can tell is pretty valuable." Jovie's mouth twisted, but she winked at Violet. "It was a passing fancy. Or maybe a passing wish. I have been finding the gents in my general association to be extremely wanting. I suppose I was hoping for the marvelous hand of fate."

"I don't blame you for being interested in this group of friends. It's not just Hamilton who's a good friend to have. We all are." For good measure, Violet added, "Me especially. I'm wonderful. A joy to the world really." Having a new victim for her favorite joke was nearly as fun as seeing her twin's eye twitch when she used it again. "Well, this was a little awkward and a little fun."

Jovie choked on a laugh. "I've already decided to focus on the fun."

"I suppose we should be friends then," Vi answered as they reached the autos. They moseyed too slowly, having to pause and wait for a school group with a long string of students. Then they helped a rather confused little lady who must have been in her 80s. When they made it to their friends, they discovered that the first auto had left with the two expectant mothers and their spouses. The second auto had left with the other couple from Jovie's group of friends.

As they were getting into the final auto with Ham and

Jack, Jovie gasped and ducked down, covering her head. "Oh! Michael said they weren't coming."

"Who?" Violet looked but there was still too much of a crowd for anyone in particular to stand out, and it was obvious that Jovie did not wish to be seen.

"Gervais and Ricky!"

"Random gents? I need details."

"Ah," Jovie replied. "Are they gone?"

"Who?"

"Spoiled types, sallow faces, mean eyes."

Violet played with her wedding ring while she searched and then said, "I think you're in the clear, dear."

Jove slowly sat up, peeking to see if she was observed. "Is it safe? Can they see me? Why am I hiding? They're going where we are going. Even if I hide from them now, they'll find me later."

"The auto is moving," Ham told her. "Who are you hiding from?"

"A couple of blokes from my school days. I tend not to come to these getaways when they do."

"Why?" Ham asked, eyes narrowed. Violet could see the alert protector ready to step in.

"They seem to think I'm theirs for the taking whenever they decide they're done with their bachelor lives."

"Why?" Violet demanded, instantly disgusted and furious.

"Because everyone else paired up among our friends, so that must mean I'm theirs. Especially after Pamela and Michael got married. No one really expected that, so they lost one of their two easy resolutions for when their mother's nagging gets too much to bear. Both of them,

Gervais especially, seem to have to tow a certain line to keep the rich aunts or whoever it is funding his life."

"There's always a rich aunt, isn't there?" Vi laughed.

"If only," Jovie said. "My aunt is not nearly so generous."

Ham leaned back and closed his eyes. Jack's gaze was fixed beyond the window. They were bored, but Violet had to admit to herself that her own group of friends had become a little boring as they had settled into their lives. Lila wasn't there to enjoy the gossip with Violet and when she was, it was all babies.

"We need to have a party," Violet announced over Jovie's description of Gervais.

"Oh," Jovie said, "I—"

"No offense," Violet told Jovie, "that was quite rude wasn't it? I prefer my gossip after I've seen the victim. Preferably with the fellow right there, story at a projecting whisper that can be overheard by the subject. Also, and this part is much more important—I'm a little scattered. Lack of sleep."

Jovie nodded. "It does sound fun to—ah, schedule a table in the dining room when they'd be around and tell you all their tales. I do hate Gervais and Ricky." In a flash of mercy, Jovie asked, "Perhaps I can go to this party."

"Agreed. Maybe it'll be by the sea. Do you want to go to Lyme or Bath or Whitby?"

"Anywhere that's cooler than here."

"On that I think we're all agreed," Ham said.

CHAPTER 3

"*W*hat do you like to do?" Jovie asked as she adjusted her dress and hat from hiding.

It would take at least an hour to motor to the lodge where they were staying, and Violet was already sweltering in the auto. She motioned Jack to roll down the window and glanced at Jovie.

Almost stupidly, Violet said, "I don't know. The usual stuff."

"She writes," Hamilton told Jovie. "Pulp novels with monsters or detectives or ingénues with otherworldly beauty and innocence."

"She buys clothes." Jack smiled at Violet. "She torments her siblings, enjoys chocolate, is something of a brilliant business woman, and interferes endlessly."

"Oh!" Jovie grinned at Violet, glanced at Hamilton and announced, "I am looking for the position of a new dearest friend. Is she free?"

"Only if you don't mind her sister, sister-in-law, Lila, and Rita sharing the position."

"Do they all like each other?" Jovie asked rather seriously. "I'm a bit finished with the women around me hating each other."

Hamilton paused and then answered rather seriously as well. "I suppose we're all a bit of a family."

"So yes?" Jovie asked. That hadn't been enough of an answer. Families hated each other all the time.

Together, the others answered, "Yes."

Violet finished, "We all like each other."

"That does sound nice." Jovie shifted and stared out the window.

It was obvious to anyone who bothered to take note that Jovie was full of underlying emotions about the recent exchange. Was it because her own family was lackluster? Or perhaps there was some oddness among Jovie's friends? It wasn't as though any of them had waited for her or looked after her. Vi paused as she considered upon that. None of Vi's friends would have left any of the others behind alone.

Even, Violet thought, the gents would have been looked after. The girls would have made sure their friends were gathered up and had a ride before letting an auto leave, and the gents would have made certain it was so. Violet felt a flash of sympathy if Jovie's friends weren't of the same caliber.

Vi asked, "What about the folks you're traveling with? How long have you known each other?"

"Since our earliest days," Jovie said rather cheerily with whatever momentary sadness she had been feeling completely hidden. "Michael is my cousin through my mother. Fanny and I shared a room throughout our school days. Pamela was just across the hall from us or just down the hall. You know how it is. Lyle was Michael's roommate. We've been each other's pockets for so long I don't remember what it is like to not have them around."

That Violet could understand. Jack, however, drew her attention to the window and Violet leaned forward to see the pretty bird Jack pointed out. The conversation turned from friendships to the countryside and then to the upcoming long weekend in the country.

"I've been here at least a half dozen times," Jovie told them. "There's a rather thrilling scramble from Scafell to Scafell Pike, but it's not a good choice for the uninitiated. Lots of other excellent places to wander about and just an excess of sheep."

"Sheep?" Hamilton asked with a smirk and Jovie shrugged. "You said that rather exultantly. Are you fond of sheep?"

"I've always loved them. Baaaah is just a delightful noise for an animal to make. Do you like animals?"

Hamilton nodded. "Who doesn't? Vi has two excellent little spaniels and I've been considering getting a bulldog."

"Really?" Violet demanded, instantly knowing that she'd be finding one for Ham. "A sweet little puppy bull-dog? With the delightful mouth and a body like Denny's?"

Hamilton's expression was a little alarmed in the face of Violet's excitement. "I just need to decide what to do with the fellow when I'm working out of town."

"Leave her with us, of course. Or Beatrice. Beatrice loves dogs and misses the spaniels when I'm not about. She's got my precious ones at the moment."

"She has rather a lot to do without me adding to it."

"Ham," Violet told him seriously. "If you don't leave your dog with us when you go, I'll be offended. Or at least leave her with our staff. I love her already. Will you name her Daisy?"

"I'm getting a male."

Violet grinned at him wickedly and it seemed that Jovie could read Vi's mind for she echoed Vi's expression.

Hamilton glanced between the two of them and then at Jack.

"Don't look to me, old boy," Jack told Ham. "You know I can do nothing."

Violet winked at Ham who sighed. "Vi—"

"Holmes was an excellent name," Jack observed. "You could do something similar."

"I could have a Moriarty," Ham agreed. "What are the chances I finish the month without a dog?"

Jack and Violet didn't even bother to answer.

"What about an Irene?" Vi suggested with amusement.

"Why must it be a girl?" Ham demanded with a scowl.

"Because you're fixated on a boy."

"I had a boy dog as a child," Ham told Vi. "I had to leave him behind to go to the war and he wasn't around when I got back."

Violet clutched her chest and then she reached out, taking Ham's hand. "Moriarty it is."

"That's too hard to say," Jack interjected. "Imagine calling that name in the park or when the dog is being naughty. What about Watson?"

"Bloody hell," Ham groaned. "Isn't this my dog? What if I want to name him Rex or...or...Puck?"

21

Vi's expression was wicked again when she answered. "It's a family dog. And he'll need a sister."

Ham groaned again, head dropping back against his seat. He closed his eyes to block out Violet's mischievous grin. He wasn't able to close out Jovie's laughter.

A moment later, Jack handed Ham a lit cigarette. "I think you need this."

"By Jove, I do." Hamilton didn't open his eyes more than a sliver to light the cigarette and then he closed them again, breathing deeply. "I think your wife might drive me mad."

"She'll drive us all mad," Jack said. "It's inevitable."

"But I'll certainly put you all in a very nice home," Violet told them. "I might even keep up your cigarette supply, but only if you keep a civil tone in your mouth."

Before anyone could reply, the auto turned up a narrow road and they all shifted to look forward.

"Oh," Violet breathed and Jovie nodded happily.

"Isn't it lovely?"

It looked like the earl's country estate if it were made of logs instead of stone. It was ridiculously large with a roof of red plank and encircled with a wide, covered porch. The garden around the lodge wasn't a sculpted masterpiece but wildness contained. Violet gasped again, taking in the carved wooden gargoyles that added the most surprising charm. There was ivy growing up the side of the building towards a series of deep, wide-set windows. They looked to each have a window seat, and everything about the place proclaimed itself to be a peaceful, arboreal haven.

"I love it," Violet told Jack. "We should have one of these."

"Or you could just come visit this one like other people," Ham suggested. "Not even your father has bought a lodge and this thing is more hotel."

"She's not normal," Jovie inserted and Violet laughed. "Why would you buy one of these?"

"My father would be much more trackable if he had but one hunting lodge instead of a series of them. But we'll come back to this one? It's delightful."

Jack's grin was there at the edge of his lips and his wide shoulders shifted slightly. "If you'd like."

"She might hate it," Ham said to Jack. "We haven't even gone in yet."

"She won't," Jovie said as Violet also said, "I won't."

Jovie added, "Oh, I do need a lover who uses the phrase, 'If you'd like.'"

"Everyone does," Violet agreed, laughing at the stoic expressions on both Ham and Jack's faces.

Violet was handed out of the auto a few minutes later by Jack while Ham handed out Jovie. They both stretched luxuriously. "Is this place as wonderful as it looks?"

A breeze hit them, whipping through the trees, and Violet closed her eyes in sheer appreciation.

Jovie nodded simply. "The rooms are comfortable, the food is amazing, the walks and rambles are always delightful. It's a bit of a dip into the wholesome side of wonderful when you explore about, but then you come back to the lodge and have cocktails in hot springs and we've returned to the spoiled lives to which we've become accustomed."

"Yes," Violet told Jack, "all of that."

"You can also make an appointment with a masseuse for a massage while you're here—even daily."

Violet was already nodding. She was going to do that too. She was going to do all of those things. "Hike, long soak in the hot springs, masseuse, dinner, cocktails."

"Sold," Jovie said. "I suppose I better run on up and locate my friends. And switch my room away from them if Gervais and Ricky are nearby. I have heard Gervais's mother has been aggressively mentioning grandchildren."

"His mother?" Ham coughed out a curse and Violet agreed.

"That sound of disgust is delightful," Jovie agreed. "His mother is the provider of the allowance."

Ham's snort followed Jack and Violet into the hotel where they were greeted with cold lemonade. Violet took her glass, a seat in the massive foyer, and refused to move until she'd finished her drink. The ceilings were tall with fans circulating the air. With the large windows and the lodge standing under the trees, the place was so much cooler that Violet felt certain if she could only have a cool bath, she'd probably survive.

"Jovie darling," Violet told her. "It has been a pleasure meeting you and spending the afternoon together, but a cool bath is singing an intoxicating lullaby."

"Oh," Jovie said, "I think I hear that song myself. Dinner later?"

"Nine o'clock?"

"Delightful," Jovie said with a wink and then turned and ran up the stairs. Her spiraled hair bounced and her mustard and brown dress flipped with each skipped step.

Ham watched her go and then turned to Violet. "You make such interesting friends. It's like people just want to tell you their secrets. I'm surprised we didn't hear about her birth, her childhood, the first time her heart was broken, and what her greatest dreams are."

"It's my eyes," Violet told him. "They're very trustworthy."

Her gaze moved over him, showing a flash of her worry, and he reached out and pressed a kiss on her forehead. "I feel as though I've gained a wonderful sister."

"Careful," Violet said with a grin, "Victor calls me a pretty devil. If I'm your sister, I'm going to interfere."

Ham turned to follow the porter to his room, but paused and looked back. "Is she all right? Have you heard from her?"

Violet didn't need him to tell her that he meant Rita. Was it Vi's comment about interfering? Did he *want* her to interfere? Because Vi wanted to. "She seems down, but she's seen some amazing things."

Ham frowned. Before he got too far from her, Violet said, "You could fix that."

Ham didn't turn, but he didn't shake his head either. She glanced at Jack, who told her, "You should leave it alone."

"He loves her," Violet told Jack. He didn't reply. Her head tilted at him, but he was unmoved. "It feels like he was asking."

Jack's expression did not agree as he took her arm and started leading her after the porter with their bags. "Draw your cool bath. I'll order ices to our room."

"Send Denny some chocolate ice cream," Violet suggested. "An oversized bowl out of kindness."

"I know you were the one behind the too-small suit."

Violet grinned evilly. She turned back to Jack and

winked. "That wasn't because I care what size he is. I just like watching Lila torture him."

Jack's bemused expression seemed to question how someone so responsible and reliable had ended up bound to someone like Vi. He didn't seem to object given the change in his expression as he followed Vi up the stairs.

CHAPTER 4

*T*he Lake District might be considerably more wild than London with distinctly country fash-ions, but Vi dressed with London styles in mind. The heat, however, was Vi's first consideration. Her dress was short, sleeveless, and pale cream with matching beads enhancing it. Vi put on a long strand of pearls and earbobs but left off the rest of her jewelry. When she turned from the mirror after applying a light layer of mascara and lipstick, she found Jack nearby, looking very handsome.

"Did you open the French doors off the balcony and the window?" she asked after allowing herself the pleasure of a moment's perusal of him. "With the fan and the hour, it might actually cool off in here."

"Otherwise you won't sleep," Jack told her with a nod. "You look lovely. Even with those dark circles under your eyes."

They must have had the same internal clock as their friends, for when Jack and Violet left their bedroom, they found Denny, Lila, Ham, and Jovie just leaving their rooms.

"Hey stranger," Violet said to Jovie, "imagine seeing you here, taking the last room by this party."

"I was across the hall from Gervais and next to Ricky. I threw a tantrum about the color of the carpets and demanded to be moved immediately. Then I apologized profusely to the staff the minute my friends weren't around and bribed them nicely to move me closer to you."

"You'll learn to regret that," Denny told her. "Even if she did send my ice cream."

"Who me?" Violet asked. "Would I do such a thing?"

"Yes," Lila told Violet. "You're evil."

"A devil really," Violet agreed. "Let's go find food, please. Now that I've cooled off, I'm starving."

"Me too," Denny agreed.

"Eat your greens, laddie," Lila ordered. "You still need to slim down."

"What if we just dance the night away? I promise to be exuberant."

Lila considered and then nodded. "Approved."

He grinned at her. "This kind woman will be the mother of my children."

"She's an angel," Jovie said.

"She's a dangerous creature," Violet and Denny said in unison and then they all looked up when they heard a woman's shriek and the sound of glass crashing.

"For the love of all that is holy," Jovie muttered. "Pamela is in one of her moods."

"Pamela?" Ham asked. "Does she need help?"

"She's a viper these days," Jovie said. "It's...I shouldn't... she was a venomous handful before she was with child.

Now—" Jovie shook her head and snapped her mouth closed. "Regardless, the food here is wonderful if they have the same chef."

Jovie turned towards the stairs with her mouth precisely closed. Vi and friends glanced at each other, pressed their lips tightly, and followed.

Denny waited until Jovie was far enough ahead to whisper without being overheard. "This is fun!"

"You're evil," Violet told him.

"You're having fun too."

"I want them to throw something at each other in the dining room," Violet told Denny as Hamilton groaned. Vi glanced at Ham, smirked, and then wound her arm through Denny's. His happy giggle echoed her sentiment.

"You seem unsurprised," Ham told Jack. "The argument between the married couple? You saw that?"

"The way that wife stomped off on the train? An affair at the least," Jack said. "Did you see the way she seemed infuriated by everyone. The other wife, Jovie? Pamela Craft is certainly upset."

Violet glanced back at the two detectives and then pouted at Lila and Denny. "They ruin all our fun."

"You thought there was something brewing." Lila placed her hand on her still flat stomach. "You were spying too."

"A blind monkey would have realized there was something wrong," Denny said as he tucked Lila's arm close. "Even I saw it. The pregnant one was upset before they got on the train and it only increased along the way."

They reached the dining hall and found that their group had been combined with Jovie's. She gave them an apologetic look as they were seated among her friends.

"Oh," Lila said, "they must have realized we've adopted you, Jovie."

Jovie's look was pure gratitude as Violet and Jack accepted their combined table and their seats next to Pamela and the oblivious Lyle. Violet glanced at Jack in delight, and his eyes glinted at her with just enough humor to know he was amused at what they would be overhearing.

Ham was seated next to Jovie on one side and Violet on the other, but just nearby was one of the gents Jovie had been hoping to avoid.

"Gervais Jenkins," the bloke said.

"There are too many dead animals on these walls," Violet announced after they were all seated.

"You don't eat meat?" The man next to Jovie scoffed.

"I prefer not to look into their eyes," Violet told him. "Lady Violet. This is my husband, Jack Wakefield."

Normally Violet wouldn't bother with what was nothing more than an honorary title, but she did like to see the look of shock in someone like Gervais Jenkins's face.

"Those are glass. Not the animal's actual eyes," Gervais said and then cleared his throat and added, "my lady. No need for you to lose sleep over them."

"If only that was what I lost sleep over," Violet said, accepting the waiter's offering of wine. "I think I'm going to drown my woes, Jack. Be warned. You might have to put me over your shoulder and haul my zozzled self to my bed."

"If he doesn't, I'm sure someone will step in," Gervais said. The look on his face was lascivious with a gaze that darted to Jovie as though she should care.

Violet blinked as she registered what he said, but Jack simply shifted his shoulders and leaned forward just enough to meet Gervais's gaze. "You won't need to be stepping in with *any* of the ladies."

Gervais drew back slightly as though he hadn't realized that Jack was quite so large. The sound of Denny's high-pitched giggle was accented by the pop of another wine bottle being opened and the clink of crystal.

Gervais looked towards Denny, who lifted his glass in salute. Lila's head tilted lazily toward the man. "So, what do you do, Gervais?"

"Oh, a little of this, a little of that. I invest and manage the investments. Bring together talented people and those who'd like to invest their funds."

Violet glanced up and the devil in her made her ask, "Really? For what companies?"

"Oh, you wouldn't understand." Gervais sipped his wine before he added, "It's all quite complicated, especially for a lady such as yourself. What do you do, Jack?"

"When I'm not watching my wife manage and invest her vast fortune?" Jack paused. "I work for Scotland Yard."

"You're a constable?"

"Jack investigates murders and other crimes," Denny announced. "For fun. Lila and I are quite lazy, but Lady Vi works enough for us all. When she's not *investing* and *managing fortunes*, she writes pulp novels."

"Surely, you're joking," Gervais said with a shout of a laugh.

"Haven't you heard of Violet Carlyle and her twin, Victor? They're the ones who inherited that huge fortune and caught all those killers and write those books?" Jovie looked as if she were having nearly as much fun as Denny. "Gervais, boyo, Lady Violet manages investments that make yours seem like mere wisps of nothing."

"You're joining in on the joke, Jovie? I thought you were one of us."

"We've adopted Jovie," Denny announced just to irritate Gervais more than anything else. "It's settled. She's ours now."

"Because this one thinks she's pretty?" Gervais asked, jerking his thumb at Hamilton. "Are you another author or a Yard man?"

"Oh, I work for Scotland Yard," Ham replied. "Jack is my subordinate."

"Another hobby detective like the lady's husband?"

"No," Ham said, smoothing his beard. "I'm quite fully a Yard man in earnest." Ham's expression was penetrating at he glanced over Gervais. Despite Gervais's higher class, Ham was the far more powerful one in the moment.

Jovie glanced at Violet, lifted a brow as if to ask, 'You see what I mean about Ham versus my friends?'

Gervais scoffed a little, glancing about for support and not finding it when he asked, "I suppose you're looking for a rich wife like Jovie to save you from Scotland Yard?"

Ham's eyes glinted and Vi winced. Denny giggled, but it had turned nervous. It was Jovie who saved the moment.

"Gervais, darling," Jovie laughed with her wicked grin and evil expression, "how would that be any different from you? I assure you that no woman would object to an honorable man like Hamilton Barnes. Indeed, wealthy women would rather have an honorable working man like Ham here than a rich spoilt one who's *of their class.*"

Gervais looked alarmed as he said, "But...oy, I didn't mean it like that."

"Then apologize," Jovie ordered. "You sound as ridiculous and snobbish as my grandfather."

Gervais tipped back his glass of wine and then scoffed. "To the working stiff? I suppose your rich friend is paying your way?"

Vi cut in with a huge dash of Lady Eleanor. Vi used the same snobbish tone, the same imperious expression, and the same capacity to talk about the utterly inane. "The weather today was stifling, wasn't it? I declare, I thought I was going to be baked alive on the train."

Jovie jumped in with far too much agreement, and then Lila, who deliberately turned the discussion to lady's hats, which drew in the other two ladies, and entirely left Gervais out.

As the dinner ended, the friends rose together—with Jovie—and left the dining room for the gardens that had been lit with torches.

"That's why, Vi," Hamilton told her, referring to their early conversation. She didn't need him to direct her mind back to it. Every time she talked to him since Rita had left, Vi had been thinking of their friend—his love—and he knew it far too well. Vi had gotten to the point where she'd had to fight to keep her mouth closed before she alienated him. She'd be damned if she lost both of her friends because of her mouthiness.

"You're right," Violet agreed. "You should definitely let fools like Gervais keep you *and* Rita from happiness rather than realizing that everyone who matters doesn't care about the size of your bank account to hers."

"Vi—"

"Rita wants children, Ham," Violet told him flatly. "She wants a family and somewhere to feel safe. She could marry someone like Gervais and have a family, but it would take a rare man who let her sleep easy. And an even rarer one who will take her as she is and love her anyway. Are you really going to deny her that because of pride?"

"What am I supposed to do?" he demanded. "How am I supposed to align the idea that I was raised to love and support my wife with the fact that she'd be supporting me or giving up her lifestyle?"

Violet paused, looking up at Ham. He was shorter than Jack, with a close-cut beard and stress lines across his forehead and around his eyes. He had the steady confidence of someone who had earned his mettle, and he was the type of man that any woman (with taste) would see as a catch.

"I don't know," Violet finally admitted. "I wish I could make it easy for you. You can examine the financial implications forever and the two of you can be apart and unhappy. Jack doesn't need my money, you know? But if you were to compare him and I—it wouldn't be so very different than you and Rita. Jack didn't leave me in love with him and alone."

"I—"

Vi cupped Hamilton's cheek and told him, "I love you like a brother. You're essential to Jack's happiness and therefore mine. Does it help to realize that you and Jack aren't so very different? Does it help to realize how broken I would be without him? Ham...I can't sleep without Jack. Even with him, I struggle and nothing makes me feel safer than Jack. Do you think it's different for Rita? Because it isn't. She might be an adventuress, but she's running too. She has nightmares and worries as well. Right now, wherever she is, I *promise* you, she's haunted."

"You can't know that." Ham's expression said he didn't want what she'd said to be true. His expression did not say he didn't believe her. Vi had always loved Ham's eyes. He'd looked up at her that first day she'd met him—on a train—and known her name. His gaze had been intrigued and with one glance she'd known that Jack had told his friend enough about Vi to be certain the growing intrigue between Jack and Vi wasn't one sided. In that moment, Vi had adored Ham and her affection had never waned.

"Of course I can," Violet said. "She's one of my best friends. Do you think we haven't talked about how to handle nightmares? Do you think we haven't talked about how to find peace after someone we love was killed? By someone we loved?"

"She's strong," Ham told Violet. "She doesn't need—"

"Don't be stupid," Violet snapped. "Rita Russell is strong and capable and brilliant and adventurous and funny and clever *and human.* You can't give her a fortune which she doesn't want, but you can give her safe harbor. The money means nothing. Safe harbor? Being loved for herself? A family? You're stealing all of those things from her with your pride."

"You're being dramatic," Ham said through gritted teeth.

"I swear to you on my mother's grave and on the grave of Aunt Agatha, Rita has nightmares too."

"That doesn't mean I can help."

"Fine," Violet snapped, just as angrily. "Fine. Eventually she'll get over you. Maybe she'll marry someone else. Maybe she'll continue to travel alone. But what she wants?

It's you. Speaking as a rich woman myself? An honorable man that you *know* isn't marrying you for your money, who sees you for you, who loves you despite your failings? That's without price. But rob Rita all the same."

Violet didn't stay to listen to whatever else Ham had to say. She was done with banging her head against that wall. She spun in the garden, crossed to the hotel, made her way to the bar. To her relief they had ginger wine and she requested another lemon ice. The chill of the evening had settled in, and Violet was more than willing to curl herself onto the bed with her favorite things rather than boxing Ham's ears.

CHAPTER 5

*V*iolet dressed for the next day in her coolest dress and sturdiest shoes. Jack had a look to him as they prepared to go for a ramble that said he'd been drinking rather heavily the night before. His eyes darted away from the light, and when she handed him aspirin, he took them without comment.

Vi blamed herself since she'd wound Ham up, but then she reminded herself she hadn't handed Jack cocktail after cocktail. So when Jack squinted a little too hard against the sun, she didn't do much more than contain her whistle. When he was a bit slower to take her arm as they walked down the stairs to the large dining room, she took his instead and refrained from commenting on the nightmare that had woken her five times the night before. It had been nothing more than darkness and the sound of two babies crying.

"Will Ham forgive me?" she asked over her plate of

fruit, handing Jack the hangover-fighting concoction that she'd ordered from the waiter. "You should wear a big hat to protect your eyes from the sun. Especially since you've overindulged."

Jack ignored her nagging which she deserved. "He knows you love him, Vi. He also knows you want him to be happy. He just doesn't think it's as easy as you do."

She frowned out the window, noting a trio of gentlemen disappearing into the trees. Who else was up so early? The ones who came here to actually hunt? She sighed and popped a melon into her mouth, allowing herself to savor the cool fruit. "I feel bad about what I said to Ham. I shouldn't have said anything."

"He listened to what you had to say and didn't storm off. The decision is up to him from here, Vi. Give him time."

"I keep thinking of Rita as if she were me. I realized I loved you before I had any idea of your feelings. It was torture. But, to think of not having you now? It's too painful to imagine. What if you'd let my stepmother drive you away? Or the stupid comments people made about money?"

Jack nudged Violet's cup of Turkish coffee towards her. "That didn't happen."

"But it *is* happening to Rita, and I adore her."

Jack shook his head, not clarifying what Ham had told him as the two friends drank too much. Perhaps they didn't speak at all. Perhaps they were only stoically smoking their cigars between sips of hard liquor. It seemed like something men would do. She and Lila would have picked apart their worries to pieces.

Vi yawned and then glanced guiltily at Jack.

"You were restless."

It wasn't a question, and she had been.

"I—" She pressed her hand to her mouth and yawned fiercely. She didn't want to tell him about the dream. The warmth would fade from his eyes and his mouth would tighten. His jaw would flex, and he'd quietly go about trying to help her sleep again.

Jack examined Vi, and she was afraid she had fooled no one. "I don't believe napping in beds is for old men. What do you say? Shall we put our sleeping clothes back on, curl into our pillows, and count sheep?"

Violet was utterly sure that Jack had little desire to nap. If she said yes, she'd probably slip into sleep and find him reading a book when she woke, never having napped at all. If she walked with him, he could enjoy this trip and she could sleep later.

"How about this afternoon? When it gets stifling hot?"

Jack considered and nodded. While Violet retrieved her sun hat, Jack discussed possible walking routes with the staff and she returned to find him ready to go. He was even holding two walking staffs, a basket with lunch, and binoculars around his neck.

Vi's lips twitched, but her voice was dry as she asked, "Are we ready for our safari?"

"It's an expedition, not a safari."

"You're right, of course. Safaris require lions."

Jack offered Violet a walking stick and his arm, and they left the lodge. The ramble into the woods was slow since they were looking for birds and wildlife and stopped several times to observe. As usual, Vi's favorites were the birds, but she found herself enchanted several times by the iridescent flutter of dragonfly wings. Violet wasn't sure how much time had passed by the time they'd stopped for lunch. She'd refused to bring her watch, but her stomach told her it was time to eat all the same.

Vi spread the blanket while Jack pulled pasties, egg and watercress sandwiches, champagne, and grapes from the basket. The breeze was cool under the trees with the shade, and she lolled happily watching the flickering of the leaves and the clouds roll by.

"Did you intend to eat?"

"But I think that one is a unicorn," Violet declared, pointing at a cloud. "You can see it if you have a believing heart."

She straightened to eat at his second nudge. By the time they'd finished their meal, Jack had leaned back against a tree and Violet was using his lap for a pillow. Sleep beckoned to her, and a part of her wondered if any chance to reset her schedule would be ruined if she succumbed. Before she could decide everything faded into shadows.

It was the sleep of a barely-aware kind. The type that happened when you couldn't quite find true oblivion. She was somewhat aware of time passing, of the feel of Jack playing with her hair, of the crinkle of pages, and the shift of the changing air, but she didn't fully rise to consciousness until she heard shouting.

She sat up suddenly and was hauled back against Jack's chest. "It's okay."

Vi blinked and rubbed her eyes. "I...who—"

"I think it's Gervais and one of the other fellows. Maybe two—"

Violet relaxed against Jack. The angry voices reached

them with the telling snideness they'd heard the night before with Gervais.

"Who do you think you are? You think you can just...just..."

The shouting changed to a long streak of cursing, and Violet pulled her legs closer to her chest.

"He'll ruin all of us! Figure it out!"

Jack's hand pressed against her stomach as if he felt sick while witnessing friends turning to enemies. She glanced up at him through her lashes and whispered, "Have you and Ham ever fought like this?"

Jack shook his head and pressed a kiss onto her forehead.

"It's like they're not even friends. They're just accustomed to being together." Violet jumped again when she heard the crack of a fist against flesh. She stiffened again. "Should we stop them?"

"They're fully grown men," Jack said. She was only a little taken aback that he wasn't intervening. They'd both faced too much harshness and violence and they were looking for a little peace, not to involve themselves in others' arguments.

Jack stood and started returning their lunch things to the basket. Violet helped, finishing with folding the blanket. Jack lifted the basket, and Violet took his hand. As they went to make their way back to the lodge, Jack asked, "Did you sleep well?"

Violet shook her head. "I was never quite unaware."

"It's like you don't remember how to sleep properly," Jack said. His gaze was far more worried than his tone, but the shouting rose again, and they hurried along.

"My brain won't stop." Violet paused as she saw movement in the trees ahead of them.

It was Gervais rushing through the wood. He seemed well and truly furious. Beyond furious. The kind of angry where you did something mad. Victor had punched a wall once when he'd been that angry. Another time had been when he'd taken their rooms and moved them out of their father's house. For Gervais? Who knew what would be possible.

Jack slowed to let Gervais get ahead and then glanced at Violet. "I think that at least Lyle and Michael were involved as well."

"Which is which?"

"Michael is Jovie's cousin," Jack said and Violet nodded. "The one married to Fanny."

"Lyle is the one married to pregnant Pamela. The one with history Jovie won't tell us about."

"Mmm," Jack agreed.

"What about Ham? Are you going to tell me what he said?"

"You seem to think that Ham and I discuss our feelings. That is not how gents work, darling."

Violet grinned up at Jack imagining the tearful conversations she and Lila had had scores of times. In this version, the memory was Ham and Jack crying and drinking instead. "Why not?"

"We just drink and smoke, Vi. It's what men do. Most of the time we don't talk at all."

"Victor will sometimes tell me things."

"Victor is far more willing to discuss feelings since he's had you wrapped around his life. Men who don't have a twin sister never discuss emotions and very rarely dreams."

Violet smirked at him. "Boys."

"Girls," he countered.

"I suppose we're all foolish in our own way. I wonder what could have gotten those men to turn on each other. Jovie said they were friends like Victor, Denny, Tomas, Lila and I. Almost more family than our own families. I can't imagine Victor punching Denny like that."

"I can," Jack said. "You'd have to be involved. Or Kate."

Violet's mouth twisted. "Did you get the picture that the blokes in Jovie's group were gallant?"

"No," Jack said, "but that doesn't mean they aren't. One of them might have been defending one of the ladies."

Violet lifted a doubting brow and she could see that Jack wasn't quite convinced, but he shrugged off the idea. They weren't there to delve into the dramas of another group of friends. They were there to hide from Lady Eleanor and maybe see if a change of scenery could help Vi sleep again.

"How do you think my babies are?"

"I think that Kate considers the girls hers."

Violet grinned. She was their aunt and the best aunt in the history of mankind, England, and the world. "I wonder how much longer for Isolde's baby. Tomas is still hiding from Father and Lady Eleanor, but I think that Isolde is being cagey about when she expects the baby to avoid having her mother there."

"Every time your sister and Tomas come back, they disappear quickly, don't they?"

"It's your fault," Violet told him. "Being the one who obeyed Father's order about not needing his daughter to swiftly wed before a grandchild appeared. When Tomas and Isolde didn't—well now, it seems to me that Tomas faces all the more trouble."

"I'd say it's Tomas's fault for not obeying," he said with amusement. Jack tangled their fingers together, hooking the basket over his arm, so he had a free hand to wind them together. "It's worked out for all concerned, however."

Violet examined the lodge as they stepped out of the trees. It was post luncheon and the windows were open to let a breeze through. It wasn't so stifling hot as the day before, but she would be happy to enjoy another cool bath again.

"There's a swimming pool behind the lodge," Jack told her. "We could go for a swim."

"Can we go at night? Doesn't that sound magical?"

"We can go whenever you'd like," Jack said, but he stopped pulling her close when they noticed yet another one of Jovie's friends arguing. On the huge porch, a hissed fight was taking place between Pamela and Lyle Craft.

"Jovie needs new friends," Violet muttered. "The rest of these folks aren't worth the breath to tell them to be quiet."

Violet laughed when Denny's head appeared from the other side of the window where Lyle and Pamela were arguing. The window was open for the heat, and Denny was skulking near the curtains. Vi was surprised the couple hadn't noticed him, but they were pretty intensely in each other's faces.

Vi shook her head at Denny, but his wide grin had her shaking off the grimness that had tried to take hold since she'd woken from her nap.

"Our friends are the best," Violet told Jack.

He squeezed her fingers. "At least they're straightforward. You'll never be surprised if he stabs you."

Violet considered the sheer idea of Denny stabbing her or anyone and laughed at the idea of it. "We need to find a way to avoid that group tonight. Jovie—"

"I already took care of it," Jack said. "Jovie has been moved to our table, which is decidedly not the same as theirs."

"You're a king among men. I'm leaving you here and finding Lila," she added.

Vi hurried up the stairs of the large porch, bypassing the arguing couple. As she went through the doors, she found an older, sporting-type couple standing just inside the main doors.

"They've been at it for a while," the woman complained to Violet. "It's ridiculous."

"We should just go out," her husband replied. "Why are we waiting for them to move or finish up?"

"I agree," Violet told him with a merry grin. "I'm positive they didn't notice me walk by or my friend listening at the window. Surely, if they saw that, they'd move. They're oblivious."

"Those two and their friends are ruining this trip," the man muttered. "I woke to them screaming at each other and the hotel staff had to come and ask them to quiet down."

"I know what you mean," Violet told them, thinking of her nap. "If you follow the trail near the willow tree it ends in a lovely meadow where my husband and I enjoyed a delightful lingering. We saw rabbits and song birds, and the bushy tail of a fox."

"Sounds better than here," the man said, firmly taking his wife's hand and nodding at Violet.

She winked at him and then said, "You mean where we hear the wild cries of the suburban housewife and her wrathful mate?"

The woman laughed and then glanced at her husband. "Just so."

CHAPTER 6

*V*iolet found Lila with Jovie. The two had taken refuge in a parlor on the second floor near their bedrooms. Lila appeared to be napping, though Violet had her doubts, while Jovie was reading a book. It took Violet a moment to see it was a V.V. Twinnings book.

"What great taste you have in your fiction," Violet exclaimed from the doorway, making them both look up. "You must be particularly clever."

"Mmm," Jovie said doubtfully, shoving back a cloud of curls, "and here I've been thinking I'm particularly stupid."

Violet's brows lifted. "Whyever for?"

"Well, I have been manipulated and nagged into spending time with Michael and friends. Over the last few days, I've come to a realization. I don't like any of them. Maybe Fanny. Michael's all right, I guess. He's my cousin, you know, so I'm stuck with him, but I would be all right if we were in people's pockets significantly less than we are."

"But you're not stuck with the rest of them," Lila said, as if she'd said it so many times she'd become bored by the idea.

"Exactly. You're so right. I'm done. This is it."

Violet glanced at Lila, who had seemed an unwilling advisor. The look on Lila's face was enough to make Vi fight a snide comment and it explained the feigned nap.

"Jack rearranged dinner seating," Violet told them. "You're with us."

Jovie paused, and Vi could see the flash of hesitation.

Lila's lazy, more unfeeling voice popped in. "You're going to have reactions to leaving your friends behind, Jovie. It's unavoidable. You've already determined this isn't the life or association you want. Change it."

Jovie's face twisted. "It's such a mess."

"Perhaps speaking of why it's a mess would help," Vi suggested.

"Tell us all the terrible details, emphasis on the sordid," Lila ordered.

Jovie glanced between the two of them. "I'll need tea."

Vi rose and crossed to the telephone, calling down for a hefty afternoon tea to be delivered to the parlor. While they waited, Jovie asked Violet about the day. She started backwards with the argument on the patio, the rumors of the argument that morning, and then the argument in the woods.

"Who was in the woods?"

"I don't know," Violet said. "Gervais most certainly, as we saw him leaving. Jack thought Michael was involved, too. Lyle was on the large porch, but he could have come from the woods. Jack and I didn't hurry back. Someone in a rage might have arrived quickly. Or maybe, he wasn't there at all. Maybe he was fighting with his wife instead."

"Who can tell?" Jovie answered exhaustedly. "They have always been fated to trouble."

"Why?" Lila demanded. "The sordid details, please."

"Oh, it is sordid," Jovie replied. She started to explain, but the tea had arrived, so they waited until the servant had left.

Violet made herself a milky tea with extra sugar and then loaded her plate with sweets. She'd added a solitary cucumber sandwich to pretend to be doing anything other than overindulging.

"Tell me the dirty details," Lila said before biting into a macaron.

"Well," Jovie said, glancing over her shoulder even though they'd closed the door to the small, private parlor. "When we were in school, before college, Lyle and Fanny were quite close. It seemed certain that they would be married the day after Lyle graduated from college."

Lila's slow, evil smile made Vi bite back a laugh, but Jovie didn't seem to notice.

"Fanny and Lyle had a huge ruckus. She'd discovered that he had been writing to another girl. He swears it wasn't serious. It was a pen pal from primary school, but she was furious. Hurt."

"Well he must have lied about it or never told her," Lila said reasonably. "I'd have skinned Denny for that."

"She did. She'd been invited to spend the summer hols with his family in the south of Spain. Instead, she rang me up and asked me to save her, so I invited her to join my family in the country."

"Uh-oh," Lila said, "thus enters Michael."

"I was busy that summer," Jovie said. "I'd taken a position as a temporary secretary for a woman and was working until tea time every day. Michael stepped in and took Fanny on the lake, for rambles, horseback riding, all the fun things, and they fell in love. Four weeks into the summer they were engaged, and the next summer, after Michael finished college, they were married."

"And Pamela?"

"She always wanted Lyle. He's the most charming of our friends when he wants to be, the best connected, the prize of the lads, you know? Michael is quieter. Everyone was surprised when Fanny picked Michael over Lyle."

"Michael probably doesn't have a secret female friend he writes to—" Vi raised her brows and Jovie answered the question.

"Weekly. And you're right. Michael may not have taken the firsts that Lyle took at college nor does he have quite the same career, but you can be assured of your place in his affections."

That was invaluable. And the lesson she was trying to share with Ham. Being assured you were loved for *who* and *what* you were? That was worth more than could be explained.

"So how did Lyle take it?"

Jovie paused. "Well. Fine."

"Except?" Lila demanded leaning in.

"He's always looking at Pamela or talking to her. It's uncomfortable. For everyone. As far as I know, however, he's never done anything else. Just look at her, get her attention, try to charm her."

Jack would not be all right with some former lover of Violet's lingering endlessly. Perhaps Michael didn't have strong opinions about it. And how did Fanny feel? The object of both men's affections—one the man she'd spurned who was now the spouse of one of her oldest friends. Was she unaware?

"How," Lila asked imperiously, "did Pamela end up married to Lyle?"

Jovie bit her bottom lip and winced. "There was this party..." She trailed off as though embarrassed. Lila didn't let it stand.

"How long have they been married?"

"They married all of the sudden about three months ago."

"She has to be at least five months gone," Lila said, referring to Pamela's obvious pregnancy.

"Party," Violet announced with a meaningful look. "Alcohol?"

Jovie nodded. "Drunk to an extent I hadn't seen before to be honest. I think that Lyle surprised himself."

"Surprise a few weeks later," Violet concluded.

"Mmmm. I'm afraid so." Jovie acknowledged.

"How did Lyle take it?"

Jovie rose and crossed to the window to look out. "He didn't want her. Anyone with half a wit would see he's still in love with Fanny. He married Pamela because she was pregnant and Fanny was taken."

"Ah," Violet mused, "a dash of honor in there."

Jovie shook her head and then said, "He didn't have much choice. Our families are wound together. If people realized he sidestepped that?"

"Ah, happily ever afters," Lila murmured.

"Since then?" Jovie rubbed the back of her neck. "It's been endless fighting. I think Pamela stupidly thought that Lyle would turn his heart to her if they were wed, but haven't we seen scores of couples who are married and can barely tolerate each other? He isn't even mean about it. He just doesn't want her. It's the same as before they were wed but now she expects attention from him, so she picks at him and whines."

"Pathetic," Lila said. "No man is going to suddenly think, 'Oh look, my whining wife. How did I miss her?' It's possible for her to get what she wants, but she's doing the wrong thing in every way."

"It's a sad story." Violet glanced at Jovie who hesitated just long enough for Violet to ask, "What?"

"I've always thought that Pamela wasn't as drunk as she pretended."

"She's clearly as pregnant as she intended if that was the case," Lila laughed.

Again Jovie hesitated and Vi breathed, "No!"

"She's awfully big for how far along she is," Jovie said. "I always thought that Ricky and Gervais had been dabbling with the goods."

Lila rolled her eyes. "This Pamela is a shady minx. Does Lyle know?"

"If he suspected? I think that Pamela would get beat within an inch of her life."

Vi winced. "That poor baby. Eventually he'll figure it out and then the child...it will be too easily ugly."

"You know," Lila said conversationally, "this would never happen among our friends. Are you sure you all *are* friends?"

Jovie looked away from the window and then returned to her seat. "I think that we were once. But it's all fallen apart. Too many wants, too much jealousy and competition."

Violet crossed to Lila and leaned down to put a kiss on her forehead. "Rita knows that we're working on Ham for her. Isolde knew that if we sent Tomas her way, it was because he was a safe bet for loving. Denny adores the ground you walk on, but even if he didn't, he'd never, not once, turn to one of your friends."

Lila nodded. "Jack would slay giants for you. He'd slay them for me. Well, Jovie, if you've done anything, you've made us grateful for our friends."

Jovie smiled, but she seemed a little sad as she did. "You have each other. You've had each other. I know you're being nice to me, and I'm grateful for it, but they're the ones who've known me forever. It'll never be the same if I abandon them for you."

"Jack, Ham, and Rita are new to our group of friends," Violet told her. "So is my sister Isolde for that matter, and my brother's wife, Kate. Even though we've known him since our earliest days, our cousin Algernon isn't among the group in the same way. It's not just about how long we've known one another. It's about choices, actions, and affections. We love Algie, but he chooses to spend most of his time with other people and doesn't quite click among us. Do what you need to do, Jovie, but don't think that we won't accept you simply because you're new."

"Really?" Jovie sighed. "While I'm baring all my terrible secrets, I don't get along with my family. I don't have anyone but my friends. If—"

"I'm afraid that as far as we're concerned," Violet interrupted Jovie, "it's an either-or situation. We can be as much of friends as you need, but we aren't going to be your buffer for that pack of lunatics you're traveling with."

Jovie sighed and then announced rather dramatically, "I didn't realize what a coward I am. I think it's time to accept that I am not what I imagined myself to be."

"You're right," Violet told her. "You should definitely accept being afraid and marry Gervais when he bothers to ask for you even though he might have parented Pamela's baby, and then spend the next several decades despising every moment with him."

Jovie shuddered. "You paint a terrible picture."

"Rise up, my friend. Create your own fate."

Violet didn't have time to listen to Jovie waffle. Vi liked Jovie, but the endless exhaustion was riding Violet and she was growing irritable, to say the least.

CHAPTER 7

*J*ovie knocked on the door of Jack and Vi's suite early the next day. Jack had left with Ham, who was acting as though she hadn't tried to persuade him to set aside his pride and chase Rita down, wrap her up in his arms, and kiss her senseless.

"Jovie," Violet greeted as she opened the door. She had been making notes on an idea for a new book, and Jovie's arrival snapped Violet out of another world.

"I—" Jovie's head tilted. "Are you all right?"

"I don't sleep these days. So no. But also, yes. I'm fine. I was just thinking about my next book."

Jovie seemed confused again, but she shook it off. "What an odd thing. Are the characters in your head like your friends?"

Vi considered and then shook her head. "When I know them well, it's like I can slip into their skin as I write them. But no, they're not fully real to me. I wish they were sometimes."

"Fascinating. I was able to schedule massages for you, Lila, and me—if you'd like to go."

Violet nodded and followed Jovie to gather Lila, who had been reading in her room.

"You're expecting a baby?" Jovie asked as they took the lift down to the baths section of the lodge. There was a swimming pool in the cellars along with several hot baths, saunas, and private rooms for massages.

"So it seems. Our friend was quite ill when she was expecting, so I keep waiting to be miserable, but so far I just want to nap more."

"A fate that she loves," Violet told Jovie. "Lila loves napping like Denny loves chocolate."

"Like Violet loves clothes."

"I do love clothes. I need a new dress, I think."

"Of course you think that," Lila said. "How many dresses do you have that you haven't worn yet?"

"Only four or five," Vi said with a laugh.

The baths were tiled in black and white from floor to ceiling with occasional bursts of color in mosaics of sunbursts and flowers. Violet followed Jovie, who greeted several of the staff by name as they reached partitioned areas with tables for massages, separated by heavy curtains. Violet took the one she was directed to and dressed in the robe that had been provided. She left her underthings on but was otherwise unclothed, which was why the whispered conversation the next curtain over with a man *and* a woman left her concerned.

Surely this was a woman's area? Vi hadn't asked before she'd disrobed, but she thought back. Yes, of course, it was. There had been the main swimming pool in the basement, and they'd bypassed that area and stepped through the double doors with the desk and the uniformed woman sitting behind it.

Vi hadn't bothered to read the sign, but she was *certain* that it had said something about this being the Ladies Area all the same.

Violet tucked the lush bathrobe about her more tightly and rose to peek through the crack in the curtains. On the other side, she found Fanny weeping in Michael's arms.

"Why didn't you tell me?" he demanded, a low level rage burning hot enough to make even Vi uncomfortable.

"What was I supposed to say?" Fanny whispered brokenly. "What was I supposed to do?"

"Tell me!"

"I—" Fanny shook her head. "He's your best friend. Since your earliest days. How many times have you told me that you are closer than brothers? That you rely upon him?"

The words seemed to be a dagger wound with each syllable. "Fanny." His voice was a breath of agony. "There is nothing that I love more than you."

It was clear the words weren't a comfort to Fanny. There was a rustle behind Violet that had her turning. A woman stepped into the curtained area, observed Violet eavesdropping and then lifted a brow.

"Mrs. Wakefield?" the woman asked.

Her voice was sufficient to have Michael Browne cursing and leaving his weeping wife behind. The harsh word had the masseuse gasping and she spun, leaving Violet alone in the partitioned room.

Violet heard the ruckus as the masseuse called, "There can be no gentlemen in this part of the baths! You must leave at once!"

Violet heard another curse and the sound of heavy footsteps moving along the tiles. The masseuse returned a moment later. "Did you see who it was?"

Violet shook her head. Michael Browne was no Peeping Tom trying to get a glance at naked ladies. He was a man having an intense interaction with his wife. They had, the both of them, seemed heartbroken.

What had happened? What had caused that break? They weren't even angry with each other. That much was clear. They'd been hurt, yes. They'd been at an impasse. They'd been tortured by whatever their break had been, but their love had been palpable.

It had felt, Violet thought, similar to what she and Jack would experience if they'd had a truly awful break. Violet winced at the idea and was struck by a flash of sympathy she hadn't been feeling for Fanny.

That comment...Violet slid onto the massage table at the direction of the masseuse and lay face down while the masseuse worked. That comment...the one about being closer than brothers. Had Fanny been keeping something from Michael about Lyle?

Vi winced.

"You must relax," the masseuse said. "I won't hurt you."

Violet took a deep breath in and then tried to release it slowly. It wasn't helping. The masseuse's own deep breath followed, but Violet ignored it and tried to think relaxing thoughts.

After a half hour, she told the masseuse, "I think that's all for now. I'm not going to be able to relax enough for you to do any good, so I'd best not waste your time any longer."

Violet rose after the masseuse left. She dressed and

then left, hurrying back to the suite. Had enough time passed for Jack to return? She found her way to their room and waited until he did, alternating between pacing and sitting.

He came back before tea and as he opened the door, Violet rose, staring at him.

"Vi?"

She answered by rushing across the room and jumping at him, wrapping her arms around his neck. She pressed a fervent kiss on his cheek and then another on his lips. Jack finished the kiss by kissing her once again and then a time after that.

"Are you all right, Vi?" His concern was evident by the way he was studying her.

She pulled back from his face. "I overhead Michael and Fanny speaking to each other."

"Another fierce spousal argument?" Some of his concern abated.

Vi shook her head. "It was heartbreaking. You could feel their love, but the pain was worse, and it made me think...we could be there someday."

Jack frowned at her, his brows dropping low as he tilted her face towards his. "Did they step out on each other?"

"I don't think so. It was like she'd been keeping something from him and he found out."

Jack brushed a kiss along her forehead. "Then don't keep anything from me that would hurt me. And I won't either. We'll just learn from them, shall we?"

Violet pressed her face into his chest and breathed him in. The scent of him and the beat of his heart gave her a comfort like little else did. Her nightmares had extended

59

to an unholy degree after the death of his uncle. Jack and his uncle had the same eyes, and watching the light leave those eyes had haunted her every single dream since. When you added in the recent risk to Violet's twin nieces, it was as if the world had conspired with her already-fervent imagination to make sleep impossible.

Jack let his chin rest against her head as he often did, and Violet said, "I promise. Even if it's horrible, I'll tell you."

"We're stronger together, Vi. Just like you and Victor. The reason our friends are family instead of near-enemies like Jovie's is that we put each other first."

Jack still held her off the ground from where she'd thrown herself at him, and he carried her to one of the sofas in the room. They sat for a long while holding each other. There was something about reveling in *not* being Fanny and Michael. In not having made the same mistakes that they had.

Jack's hand pressed against Violet's back, and they were murmuring together about the most random of things. The most recent book they'd both read. The dinner they'd had the previous evening where the beef and mushrooms had been cooked in the most divine of red wine sauces. The color of little Vi Junior's eyes changing from blue to deep brown like Violet's own. The way that little Agatha watched Kate with a preternatural awareness of the whereabouts of her mother, but the way both girls lit up when Victor spoke.

"Do you think that they heard him while they were still within Kate? That his voice was something that they found comforting before they even joined us?"

"Possibly," Jack said. "Just in case, when we decide to

have a baby, I shall have to talk to him or her often, so my voice will work as magically as Victor's does on the twins."

He spoke of other bits of information he'd learned about the area, and the murmur of Jack's voice was sufficient to allow her to relax enough to slip into oblivion, which rarely happened when it was actually time to sleep. So it was that they lingered far past the dinner gong with Violet sleeping without dreams. The moon rose high when she finally woke.

"I've been thinking," Jack said as though she hadn't just slept hours in his arms, "we really should have gone sailing. A yacht would have let us avoid this pack of fools."

"We could control who entered our environment," Violet agreed as she pushed back from his chest and glanced up at him. She pressed her hand to her mouth and found she'd been slobbering a bit. "Oh, my. I'm sorry."

Jack's laughter had her grinning.

"How late is it?"

"Rather late. We've missed dinner and then the time for dancing after. I fear the kitchens are closed if you're hungry."

Violet was hungry. Her eyes glinted with mischief. "We could do a little breaking and entering."

Jack's eyes brightened with an echo of her mischief. "Perhaps a midnight picnic by the pool?"

"Yes," Violet said instantly. "Yes, of course. No better idea has ever been uttered."

CHAPTER 8

*T*hey changed into bathing costumes, topped themselves with the luxurious robes the lodge had provided, and left their bedroom. The lights were low in the hallway with every door closed. No sign or sound of any of their friends said they were doing anything other than sleeping.

Jack led the way, pausing at the intersections of the hallways as though they were doing something illicit. Violet followed silently in his wake through the halls, bypassing the main desk where a uniformed man was at the ready to assist anyone in the nighttime hours. Jack just lifted a hand to the man and kept going.

The hallway down to the kitchens shifted from the overt luxury of the guest area to the utilitarian cleanliness of the staff areas. The kitchens were not locked, and it took only a few minutes to locate biscuits, bread, cheese, and wine. They took their booty and hurried out the back door before they were caught.

Vi was laughing as the dark grounds of the lodge rolled out before them. "I haven't been to the pool yet. Have you?"

Jack shook his head but said, "I walked past it yesterday with Ham. He gave me a message for you on our ramble today."

"Did he?" Vi asked as they stepped onto the path leading from the lodge. It was dark, but the lodge had left a few of their gas lamps burning.

The pool itself was inspiring. It had been built as though by the Romans, with columns and statues and even a pouring fountain in the center. The columns were lit by more gas lights that reflected off the still water.

"Oh, it is lovely. Look, Jack!"

"It's even better now that it's not crowded with others."

Violet sat on the edge and stuck her toes in. The chilly night air combined with the cool pool water would make this a quick swim if they didn't move fast enough to heat themselves up.

"We need one like this. With a theme. More than just a hole in the ground with water. Something that is lovely in and of itself."

Jack sat next to her, wrapping his arm around her waist. "Do you want to hear the message?"

Vi looked up, distracted from the water. "Yes, of course."

"He said to tell Rita in your next letter that he regrets everything except the last thing he said."

Vi gasped and twisted towards Jack. "Does that mean what I think it does?"

His eyes moved over her face with enough weight that

it felt almost as though he were trailing his finger over her skin. "I think so."

"Do you think…"

"Do I think that he loves her, regrets not taking her in his arms, and kissing her senseless?"

Violet nodded.

Jack's answer was to take her in his arms and kiss her senseless.

When they could both breathe again, he said, "I told him that the biggest regret of my life was not telling you I loved you sooner."

Violet hadn't known that such a simple statement, one that she already knew to be true, could bring her to tears, but it did. They welled up in her eyes and she kissed him to fight their escape.

"What's all this then?" Denny asked from behind them. "Romantic getaways. Affection in public. These bright young things, Lila. They have no respect. No under-standing of modern values."

"True," Lila said idly as she stepped into the light. "I have never been so disgusted. Animals. Someone call a vicar and make these amoral *creatures* listen to the good word of the Lord."

She crossed to their pile of pilfered goods and added to them. "We've brought chocolates, tinned biscuits, and champagne."

"I want some of that dinner we had yesterday," Violet said, pulling away from Jack. "I'm going to eat such a mountain of breakfast tomorrow."

They sliced the bread and cheese and followed it with wine and chocolate and then Violet was the first to drop her robe and dive into the water. A quick secondary splash told her that Jack had joined. Lila's high-pitched gasp and Denny's squeak said she and Jack weren't alone. Vi quickly wrapped her legs around Jack's waist from behind, crawling up his back to dive upon Denny and pull him under.

They played like children until Jack said, "Vi, your teeth are chattering."

Lila's laugh cut off with its own chattering, and Denny hopped out of the pool with his entire body shivering. "Why aren't you freezing, Jack? Are you impervious to the cold?"

"Yes, well, you know us heroic types. We don't feel the heat or the cold."

Violet wrapped the robe around her wet bathing costume and wrapped a towel around her hair. Both the thick robe and fluffy towel warmed her at once. She threw Jack's robe to him and noticed the shiver as he wrapped himself. "What time is it?"

"At least 3:00 a.m. Maybe 4:00."

"You know what that means, don't you?" she asked.

He shook his head at her as he slid his feet into his shoes. They gathered up the remnants of their stolen feast as she added, "Breakfast, hot coffee, tea, chocolate. Something warm. We'll want something cold later to keep us confused."

"Summer is the worst," Denny announced. His arm was wrapped around Lila and he pressed a kiss against her forehead. "This was fun. You definitely need a pool. Then we can do this without all these extraneous guests."

"I know," Violet said. "We *are* spoiled."

"I prefer things that way," Denny admitted. "This lodge is great. That old couple, the ones you talked with, Vi, they're great. I want to be them when I grow up."

"But they were going out for a ramble," Violet pointed out. "Surely by then, Lila will have lost her battle against your bulge, and you'll be unable to walk farther than the dining room."

"Vi!" Denny moaned. "Is that what you think?"

He was at the forefront of their little group, leading the way towards the lodge from the pool that wound through the more sculpted part of the garden. He spun around to Violet, walking backwards as he asked, "Vi? Really?"

"Denny," Lila told him sweetly, "your dad is quite large and you have the same bad habits."

"Bloody hell," he muttered, coming to a halt.

"Just move," Jack told Denny. "It's not that difficult. Go for a swim, do some rowing, play tennis. Find one activity you hate least and do that more."

"Really?" Denny asked. He slowly began walking backwards again. "My father is quite large. He can't walk without losing his breath."

"Yes, exactly," Lila said dryly.

"I can, however, walk backwards without losing my breath." He grinned then twisted to face forward and stumbled, hitting the ground hard.

Jack laughed while Lila gasped and Violet winced. Lila stepped over to Denny, hesitated, and the scream that followed was horrifying.

Jack pulled Violet back as he rushed forward, but Violet was a breath away from him as she followed.

"Holy madness," Denny groaned, trying to get his knees under him. "What was that?"

"A body," Lila said, breathless. She gingerly stepped around the prone shape and dropped down next to Denny. "Are you all right?" Her concern was readily apparent, a strong reminder of the love she and Denny shared that not everyone noticed past their playful idleness.

Violet stepped around Jack, avoiding the body to give Denny a hand up. He pulled Lila up with him and the two of them looked down while Violet very carefully looked away. She had no desire to add to her nightmares.

"Dead or hurt?" Vi asked cautiously.

"Dead." Jack's grim voice told Violet more than she wanted to know.

"Ham?"

"Please. Not alone."

Vi glanced at the others and Lila took Vi's hand. "We've got this."

They took off at a run and Lila kept pace with a speed Vi was surprised she was capable of. They reached the lodge and Violet called to the man at the desk, "Call for a doctor. Immediately." She didn't wait to hear his reply, and with Lila next to her, she ran up the stairs, bypassing the lift to rush down the hall towards Ham's room and bang on the door. He opened the door a minute later and took in her expression.

"Bad?"

"I didn't look."

"Yes," Lila said, resolutely.

"Murder?"

"Yes," Violet and Lila said in unison.

"Damn it," Hamilton replied. He kissed Vi on the cheek and said, "Stay with Lila." Lila got a kiss on the cheek and an order to stay with Vi. Then he shut his door to exchange his pajamas for a suit. When his door opened again, they were across the hall in Jack and Vi's room with the door opened to watch for him.

"We told the deskman to call for a doctor," Violet said as he shut his door.

"He should call the local constables as well."

"So tell him to," Lila told him.

Ham grinned at them, then sobered. "Lock the door." Before he made it three steps, Jovie's door opened. He studied her, then nodded toward Lila and Violet. "Stay with them. Lock the door. Don't open it until Denny gets back here and then stay together."

Lila nodded. Jovie hurried across the hall with Ham's order spurring her on without question. Those would inevitably come. Violet closed the door behind Jovie and locked it. She leaned her face against the wood as Lila cursed and crossed to the decanter in the corner. Vi heard the clink of the glass and called, "Pour me one."

"Oh, we're all getting one."

Violet slowly turned to face the baffled Jovie and the ghostly-white Lila, who handed Violet a glass with a shaking hand. Vi took it and crossed to the window, looking down to see an auto pulling up. Several staff members had been called outside, and then Vi noted the constable's auto moving up the long drive.

"Those poor fools," Violet said. The nearest town had to be tiny. These constables were prepared to deal with noise complaints and drunks. If they were smart, they and their commander would ask for Scotland Yard and Ham would be assigned. "We're never going to get a real vacation."

"We're cursed," Lila added as she sipped her drink. "Jack only smokes cigars now?"

Vi nodded.

"I want a cigarette."

"We're not leaving the room."

"*What*," Jovie asked in exasperation, "is going on?"

"Body," Violet said. "On the path."

"Are they all right?" Jovie demanded.

"Oh, the poor lamb," Lila muttered.

Violet would have laughed, but it wasn't funny. None of this was funny. The body on the path. The way they kept tripping over dead people. The terrible things that people do to each other. Always for some terrible reason. Money or because they loved the same woman or one parent more than the other. Greed when things were given fairly and the eldest wanted more than the fair share. The desire for the same promotion. To keep the child you loved trapped at home. Better dead than with their unapproved lover.

Vi knocked back the glass Lila had poured and gasped against the burn.

"What happened?" Jovie asked again.

"Murder," Violet told her. "It's always murder."

"Always?" Jovie's elfin eyes flicked between the two women. "How could you possibly mean that? There's a body? Someone was hurt? Has the doctor been called? Why are we locked away?"

"The poor, sweet, innocent lamb," Lila repeated, taking Vi's glass to refill it.

"Murder is the only conclusion for a body on a path."

"What about an accident or a health concern?" Jovie demanded. "How could it be anything *but* an accident?"

Lila handed Violet a full glass and said, "Because we're here."

"Jack wouldn't have sounded so grim if it wasn't obviously a murder."

"It was obviously a murder," Lila said, sipping her drink again. Her color had not improved and Violet was concerned for the baby. But Kate had made it through more than one murder and the twins had survived. Surely it would be the same for Lila's baby.

"How do you know it was *obviously a murder?*" Jovie demanded.

"I saw the body." Lila had wrapped both hands around the glass, the gesture revealing how unsettled she was regardless of how she kept her tone calm, even bored.

"Who was it?" Jovie demanded.

Vi shuddered.

"You'll know eventually," Lila told Violet gently.

With her fingers pressed against her eyes, Violet nodded.

"Lyle Craft."

Jovie gasped and Violet shook her head against the assault of images.

"How?" Jove demanded.

Vi shook her head. She didn't want to know. Not yet.

"I slept after tea," Vi told Lila.

"I know. We peeked in on you."

"It was lovely," Vi groaned. "I felt like I could fly after I woke up."

"I don't understand," Jovie complained.

"Stick with us, and you will," Violet said. She crossed to call down to the desk for tea. It was rude and at a terrible time when the staff would have more to deal with than was fair, but she didn't care. She ordered the tea, ignoring the apologies about a delay and just requested that it come with scones, fruit, and the usual accoutrements.

CHAPTER 9

"*L*yle!" Jovie sat down suddenly. "That couldn't be a health problem. I suppose it could have been an accident."

"It was not an accident," Lila said flatly. Her face, tone, and color made it clear that Lyle's death had been ugly.

"How do you know?" Jovie demanded.

"Don't," Vi said. "Don't. I don't want to hear the details. You don't either, Jovie."

"I do! He was my friend. Of course I want to know. I *need* to know."

"You don't," Violet shot back, but her voice was gentle in its fervency. "You don't want to know *because* he was your friend."

Violet rose and crossed to the window again, staring out and seeing the constables scurrying about.

Jovie stood suddenly. "Someone has to tell Pamela and the others."

"No."

"The poor lamb," Lila added.

"Why are you saying that?" Jovie cried. "My goodness. Lyle? Are you sure?"

"Yes," Lila pressed her hands to her face. "I might be taking a page out of your book for the next few days, Vi."

"What does that even mean?"

"Nightmares," Lila and Violet replied.

"We still need to tell my friends."

"We aren't going to do any such thing," Violet said, still gently.

Jovie glanced between them and then there was a knock on the door. Violet and Lila both froze until they heard, "Room service!"

Violet crossed to the door, peeked out, and noted the uniform and the loaded tea cart.

"They hate you right now," Lila told Violet, who couldn't help a dry laugh as she opened the door.

"Dig some money out of Jack's billfold," she ordered Lila. "It's there on the bedside table."

Lila pulled out more than they'd normally tip, but it was very early.

"Why can't we tell my friends?" Jovie demanded as Violet shut the door and locked it once more.

Vi studied her new friend. Jovie's hair was bound by a wrap, her pajamas were a deep royal purple, her eyes had lost their spark, and there were circles under them that proclaimed she hadn't had enough sleep.

"Jovie," Violet told her. "One of your friends killed Lyle."

"What? No. Perhaps some sort of...of..."

"Don't say it," Lila said. "It's never the servant or the tramp or the passing gypsy or whatever it is that people like to claim. It's always the friends. The lover or the betrayed best friend or the son or the cousin or the heir, but never the tramp."

Jovie stared at Lila's clear certainty before facing Violet, who nodded wearily.

"Let's change." Violet dug through her bags until she found her extra kimono and a pair of pajamas and tossed them to Lila. They took turns changing. Violet was running a brush through her hair when Jovie found her voice.

"Never?"

"Never," Violet said clearly. No good would come from giving Jovie hope that anyone but an acquaintance had killed her friend.

There was another knock at the door and Violet crossed and found Denny. His hair was wet, he was out of his robe and dressed for the day, and she recalled as she opened the door that he'd fallen over a body.

"Bloody hell," Violet said, examining him for the remains of blood that must have been on him.

Lila stepped up behind Violet and pulled the door from Vi's grasp to let Denny in. Lila handed him her drink. "Good, you washed."

"Three times," Denny admitted. "It was horrible."

"Stop please," Violet said. "Save the telling details for when I'm not around. I've already heard too much to be able to sleep for the next several months."

"I don't understand," Jovie said.

"This has happened too many times," Lila replied. "Why we always have to have a front row seat, I don't know."

"We're cursed."

"Obviously."

"What's happening?" Jovie asked, glancing among them like they were crazy.

Denny crossed to the teacart to load up a plate and sat down with an exhausted sigh.

"They're taking pictures of the body and looking around the scene for clues," Violet explained to Jovie. "As soon as they have what they need, Hamilton, possibly Jack, and one of the local detectives will go and knock on Pamela's door. They'll tell her about Lyle and then they'll start searching and questioning."

"For what?" Jovie asked, glancing between them with wide, horrified eyes.

"The murder weapon," Denny told Jovie without sympathy. They were, all of them, becoming inured to it. "Evidence that one of your friends killed him. They'll try to find footprints or signs of a scuffle on one of you. They'll look into your financials and the rumors and all the things that were happening between you."

Violet watched the horror on Jovie's face as she realized what they were trying to say.

Her voice was hoarse as she asked, "You really think one of my friends killed Lyle?"

"Yes," they all said.

Jovie took the tea that Lila made her, dumped the remnants of her bourbon in the tea and then sipped it slowly. "Which one?"

None of them answered.

"Regardless of whoever it is," Jovie said, "all of our secrets will be poured out and examined."

There really wasn't anything to say about that either.

Jovie watched in horror while Denny woodenly ate a

scone with clotted cream and jam. It was overloaded with both, just how he liked it, and Vi was sure he wasn't tasting it. Not really. Lila watched Denny eat, holding his hand.

Jovie finally seemed to come to herself. "It doesn't seem possible. He was just alive," Jovie said, pacing with Vi. "I was thinking how much I disliked him at luncheon when he made some comment about Pamela having become larger than he expected."

Denny winced.

"Did she cry?" Lila asked.

Jovie nodded. "Pamela has always been quite vain."

"Denny," Violet advised, "don't make the same mistake."

"I never would. Lila loves me round. How could I not love her when our baby is growing within her? That's just…magical."

"It is, isn't it?" Vi crossed to Lila and wrapped an arm around her, laying her head against her shoulder. "Little Vi and Agatha are my bright lights. That's what you're doing, making a bright light."

"Let's not get too hasty," Denny said with that mischievous light in his eyes. "Geoffrey is your stepmother's bright light."

Vi winced as Jovie asked, "Who is Geoffrey?"

"My little brother, the wart," Vi answered absently, crossing to the window again. She caught sight of Jack's large silhouette squatting near the ground. There were lanterns out there now, their bright light circling the ground.

Vi would guess that they were searching for a murder weapon. Someone would be taking pictures of the body.

The police would be hoping to recover whatever they could from where the crime had happened, whatever hadn't been destroyed by Denny falling over the body and the rest of them walking blithely around in the dark as though the world weren't a horrible place where longtime friends murdered and betrayed each other.

"Vi," Jovie asked, reaching out and taking her hand, "are you all right?"

Vi shook her head. No. Of course she wasn't. None of them were. They were, all of them, not all right. Perhaps being all right would come again. Perhaps, in the coming weeks, they'd wake up and realize that it was a beautiful day and what had happened wasn't their fault.

That day wasn't, however, today.

"What do we do?"

"We can't trust any of them," Violet told Jovie. "It doesn't matter what you think you know and who you think you can trust. You can't."

"Is that how you would feel if it were Denny lying dead and your friends as suspects?"

"No," Violet told Jovie bluntly. "But we've already established that my friends are not your friends. When Denny had to go to Hong Kong for a year for his work, Victor and I took Lila with us. Victor didn't romance her, but he did distract her. We wrote Denny letters about how she was and took her to the earl's grounds with us. We got Aunt Agatha to bring us all to the sea. When Victor and I were called home to face family ruckus and trouble, Lila and Denny came and they were who we could trust when everything seemed ruined."

Jovie's lips quivered.

Violet continued. "When my cousins were all suspects

and my aunt lay dead, Lila and Denny didn't flee. In all the madness we've seen since, none of us has abandoned the other. Your friends have been turning on each other. You already wanted to avoid them. It's over, Jovie."

Her eyes were shining as she whispered, "It has been for a while, hasn't it?"

Denny nodded.

Violet didn't know what else to tell Jovie. Vi didn't believe in a version of events where all went well. Not anymore. She was….it was so much more than tired. She was soul weary. It seemed there was a level of having something horrible happen to you time and again that calloused you to the terrible thing happening. What did Jovie have to whine about, Violet thought, hating herself for thinking it. Jovie had only lost one friend who wasn't really a friend.

Another thought struck Vi a moment later. In all the times she'd lost a friend or discovered a body or gotten sucked into another case, she'd never been alone. Empathy burned through her as she crossed to Jovie. "Losing someone you know is terrible. It's terrible when you know that one of your friends is the likeliest killer and that in the coming days one of them will be uncovered for what they did. You'll discover the nature of your friends in ways you didn't want to know."

"You sound like you're trying to comfort me, but the things you are saying…"

"No one gets what you're going through like we do, Jovie. You aren't alone."

Jovie glanced among them. "What do I do?"

"Be kind to your friends, but maybe don't be alone with them."

Jovie's watery laugh was echoed by Vi's. "This is horrible."

Vi nodded and added more bourbon to Jovie's tea. "When my aunt was murdered, I thought I could understand. I thought I could move past it. I couldn't, but I thought maybe. Then my sister's fiancé died. I stumbled over his body and my twin got me thoroughly drunk afterward. I hated him. The fiancé, I mean. I adore my twin."

"And then?"

"Then it was a money-chasing woman who thought to entice another of my friends into marriage. Then a man who obsessed over and murdered a girl we knew...I could go on, but I don't want to. It doesn't get easier."

"Why are you telling me this?" Jovie asked, dismayed.

"It doesn't get easier, but friends make it easier. You aren't as alone as it feels. And maybe, at the end of this, when you've witnessed the true nature of your friends, you'll be more settled about the choices you make for the future."

Jovie's mouth twisted and she curled onto the end of Vi and Jack's bed. Jovie didn't so much weep as silently watch the movement of the lights outside. The sun began to rise and the lanterns disappeared.

They heard a scream.

"Pamela," Jovie said.

Violet closed her eyes. Perhaps the relationship between Pamela and Lyle had been injured and broken, but it was a marriage. Perhaps she had loved Lyle. She was —possibly—carrying his baby, but she had received news that would change the rest of her life.

"Poor Pamela," Jovie said. She hadn't cried for Lyle on

her own, but the sympathy tear that rolled down Jovie's face was quickly followed by a flood. Violet rubbed Jovie's back as she sobbed, and they all waited for Jack or Hamilton to arrive. They couldn't stay locked in the bedroom forever, but Violet had little doubt that the orders for her safety and Lila's would reach them quickly.

CHAPTER 10

"*D*on't go anywhere alone," Jack told Violet.

His gaze moved from her in a clear, overt order to Denny and Lila. The command was nearly as strong to them and then his gaze moved to Jovie. Vi knew him well, so could see the doubt in his eyes. Jovie hadn't been swimming with the rest of them. She might have no reason to kill Lyle that the rest of them could see, but she wasn't well and truly out of Jack's suspicion.

"Are you concerned that whoever killed Lyle will kill someone else?" Jovie asked.

"We don't know *why* Lyle was killed yet," Jack told Jovie. He had changed out of his damp bathing costume and into his customary suit. "The chances of the killer being a madman who intends on killing repetitively is unlikely. Most people don't kill indiscriminately. But if they are murderers, they'll kill again to hide their crime. All it takes is you discovering the killer getting rid of their bloody clothes, and you'll die too."

Jovie's gaze was wide and horrified. "So you're saying I can't trust any of my friends?"

"I wouldn't," Jack told her flatly. "Chances are very high that one of your friends is the killer. We'll find out who as soon as we find out why."

"I can't just stay in this room, in my pajamas, while you investigate. Even if it's not safe, I don't have a choice. I *have* to check on Pamela and let my cousin know I am all right."

"Walk Jovie to her room, Denny. Lock the door, don't open it for anyone. Get dressed for the day. Violet will dress and come for you. She'll go with you to visit Pamela Craft and your cousins."

Violet had little doubt he wanted her to eavesdrop. She would have, of course, anyway, but he was slipping her right into the middle of the investigation when usually he tried to keep her out of it.

Denny took Lila and Jovie with him.

Jack approached Violet. "Are you all right?"

Obviously not, but Vi didn't want to add to his burdens, so she only shrugged. His look was unimpressed by her omission, but he knew her well enough to know what she was doing, and she knew him well enough to know she hadn't been successful. The last thing she needed was another body on her mind while she was trying to convince her own body to sleep again.

"Did you see?" he asked.

"I didn't look."

Jack cupped the back of her neck and pulled him into her chest. "Try not to think of it."

Vi's sarcastic laugh was sufficient to tell him how well that request would be honored. If she could stop remembering the terrible things, reliving them over and over, she'd have done so a long time ago. At least she wasn't fighting the blues as well, she thought, and then pushed up on her toes to kiss his chin.

"Have you and Ham been officially assigned?"

Jack nodded. "Ham said to tell you to consider a sea holiday as this one has shifted to work."

Vi grinned at that idea. "Ooh. Maybe we can get Victor and Kate and the babies too."

Jack pressed another kiss on Violet's forehead. "Be careful with Jovie. She trusts these people. She thinks she knows them. They will, however, speak more freely around Jovie. Hopefully they won't think too deeply about you being connected to Ham and me, especially with Jovie's reactions."

Violet nodded and then walked Jack to the door. She knew he'd stand on the other side of it until she locked it. The second she did, she watched through the peep hole as he hesitated, checked the door, and then walked away. There was a constable at the end of the hall, and Violet had little doubt that Jack was behind someone watching over their rooms.

She hurried to the bath and drew herself a hot bath with lavender oil and Epsom salts. She soaked in the water for a long time trying to *not* think of the murder. It didn't work, so she lathered her skin with soap, scrubbed her hair, and trimmed her nails. She was procrastinating, she knew. She was procrastinating because she didn't want to delve into the *why* of someone killing their friend.

Violet slowly rose from the bath. Her robe was still wet from the swim, so she wrapped herself in a large towel, wrapped another around her hair, and rubbed her skin with cream.

"Why," she asked herself aloud, "would lifelong friends turn on each other?"

She didn't have an answer. Her siblings were near strangers to her from a lifetime of boarding schools and being sent away to her aunt's, so her friends had become her family. It had to be the same for them, didn't it? Lyle and Michael, Pamela, Jovie, and Fanny, Gervais and Ricky. Probably sharing the same sports, the same lectures, helping each other on assignments, and arranging to see each other over the holidays.

When Violet asked herself why she might be driven to killing Lila or Denny, her whole body rejected the idea.

"Why?" she asked herself again. "Why?"

Then she remembered the broken sound of Fanny and Michael whispering to each other. Would Jack kill—say Denny—if he hurt Violet terribly? Perhaps not, but Jack would have to fight himself not to. Her husband was, however, an extraordinary example of honor and fortitude. Very few could say the same.

Violet sighed as she chose herself a dress. She would be sleuthing with Jovie, holding hands and listening to weeping and mourning. She'd need to keep those things in mind, but she also glanced outside. The weather was very hot for England. The skies were clear, the sun already bright, the breeze non-existent. She glanced again through her dresses before choosing a light tan with a sailor's collar and a pleated skirt.

Violet added sturdy, brown shoes and a black headband to hold back her hair. She left off all jewelry except her wedding ring. Filling her satchel with her journal, a pen, and her pocketbook, Violet considered the day ahead again.

She paused and then listed the thoughts that had been striking her throughout the morning. "Lyle could have been murdered by Michael if whatever had Fanny crying was bad enough." Violet held up a single finger. "Lyle could have been killed by whomever was going to be ruined." Being financially ruined had been the motive for more than one death, if that was the type of ruin being argued in the forest.

Her head tilted as she paced. "What if Lyle discovered that Pamela had tricked him into marriage? Could he have turned on Pamela? Maybe he did and she killed him in self-defense?"

What a terrible thought. A woman murdering her husband while massively pregnant. Vi shuddered. She couldn't help, of course, thinking of the recently pregnant Kate. What if Kate had gone mad and murdered Victor? Violet shook it off immediately. There was simply no way that Kate would ever hurt Victor. Or be successful in hurting him for that matter. Victor was no mountain of a man like Jack, but her brother could overpower Kate without an issue.

Vi sighed as she paced. She didn't want to be here or a part of these things. Maybe it was time to start embracing that her life was cursed with dead bodies and people who murdered each other. Maybe it was time to start taking back control. Perhaps if she stopped dreaming of the people she loved as victims and began dreaming of ways to stop people from getting away with these crimes, she'd be less haunted.

She glanced towards the door where Jovie was probably dressed and waiting. If Vi took too long, Jovie would go on her own. Vi had little doubt that Jovie was no cipher. She might be reeling, but who wouldn't be after being touched by murder?

Violet took a deep breath in. Don't leave Jovie alone. Don't be alone. Find some happiness. And maybe a killer.

"I DON'T KNOW what to say." Jovie was nibbling on her bottom lip, her gaze wide as she considered. "I'm sorry? That seems entirely insufficient."

Violet shook her head.

"You lost family to murder, right? Your aunt?"

Vi nodded, the pain of it striking her once again. Vi closed her eyes and told Jovie, "There's nothing you can say. Just tell her that you're sorry and mean it. Tell her you're worried about her and mean it. Be there for her while she suffers."

"There isn't some bit of wisdom that helped?"

"In the moment, I was angry. I was determined to find the killer and make them pay. Now? It still hurts. She was a mother to me, and I lost her, and every time I realize there is something else that won't be the same without her, it hurts. I'm an aunt now. I look at my nieces and realize Aunt Agatha isn't here to hold them and she won't be there for my children either."

Jovie winced as Vi wiped away a tear. With a deep breath in, Violet tried for a smile.

"But you have your stepmother, right?" Jovie asked.

Vi laughed and shook her head. "No. Indeed not. What about your parents?"

"They're gone. I was raised mostly by my aunt and uncle. I'm not their favorite, but it's not so bad. I have Fanny and Michael and—" Jovie stopped as she realized what she was saying. She did have her cousin and his wife. Assuming they weren't the killers.

Vi squeezed Jovie's hand as they went down the grand staircase to the large foyer below. "We'll be your friends."

"You don't really know me," Jovie said low. "You might not like me once you do."

Vi grinned. "We aren't that picky. Don't be a cheating liar and don't be a killer. We can deal with a fair amount of personality quirks after that. I mean...have you met Denny?"

"I like Denny," Jovie said with the edge of a sniffle.

"Which is why you fit us so well. Let's stop borrowing trouble, shall we?"

Violet glanced towards the front desk and an idea occurred to her. If not for today, then for tomorrow. She followed Jovie to a separate wing of the hunting lodge and to a series of doors where there was a police constable watching everything. Before they could knock on Pamela Craft's door, Hamilton stepped into the hall.

Ham shook his head. "Not now. The doctor is in there. She's hysterical. He's worried for the baby."

"Oh no," Jovie said. "The baby?"

"She's saying that she's feeling contractions. It's too early."

"Even if the baby isn't Lyle's it would still be too early," Jovie muttered.

"Not Lyle's?" Ham turned on Jovie just as the door to the room across the hall opened.

"What's not Lyle's?" Michael Browne asked.

87

Jovie snapped her mouth closed.

"Jovie," Ham said as gently as possible. "The time for keeping secrets is past."

"But—"

"What's not Lyle's?" Michael demanded. "What are you talking about, Jovie?"

"The baby," Fanny said from behind Michael. "Jovie doesn't think the baby is Lyle's."

Michael turned to his wife and demanded, "What? How do you know?"

Fanny hesitated. She was pale with dark circles under her eyes and the look of a woman who had been crying. If Vi didn't know Lyle had just died, she'd guess Fanny had been crying for days, but it hadn't even been a full day yet.

"I never thought the baby was Lyle's either."

"Because he was chasing you? Shadowing you? Wanting *you?*"

Fanny looked away, mouth downturned. She didn't answer, but who needed her to?

"Who do you think the baby belonged to?" Hamilton asked Jovie gently, ignoring the fraught emotions between Michael and Fanny.

Jovie hesitated when her cousin turned on her, eyes blazing.

"Did you know?" he demanded. "Did you know what he was doing to Fanny?"

Jovie shook her head, but there was just enough hesitation in it that Michael spun fully on Jovie, grabbing her arms and pushing her against the wall. "Did you know he was shadowing her? That he was…was…touching her when I wasn't around? Did you know that—"

"Let her go," Hamilton commanded, grabbing

Michael's arm. Vi didn't wait. She kicked Michael in the back of the knees and grabbed him by his ear, pulling him off of his cousin.

"Yes, obviously," Violet answered for Jovie. "She knew that Fanny was uncomfortable around Lyle. Did she know how bad it was? Obviously not. She would have told you. My goodness, man, I would have told you. But even *I* could see that Lyle was obsessed with Fanny and I've only spent a few hours with you in total. *Why* are you blaming Fanny and Jovie? Look in the mirror."

Michael cursed at Violet and shoved her off of him. He stepped closer but Hamilton growled. "Careful."

Michael cursed again and then punched the wall, breaking through the plaster before he spun and left.

CHAPTER 11

"Temper, temper," Violet murmured low, but Hamilton heard her.

"Foolishly so," he murmured back. "Does he want to be our main suspect?"

Fanny was gasping, crying into Jovie's arms. The constable had followed after Michael at Hamilton's nod. A door down the hall opened and Ricky stepped out. He took in the scene and said nothing, but he didn't leave either.

Ricky, in fact, leaned against the wall and crossed his legs. He looked as though he was prepared to be entertained. Perhaps even as though he delighted in the madness.

One of these people killed their friend, and it seemed almost as though they didn't care. Where was the rage? Where was the upset in anyone other than Fanny? Vi shuddered as she took a terrible breath in and told herself they weren't going to be victims of this madness and what had been done here. They were going to win. With her eyes still closed, Vi searched for her wits. Fanny's sobs felt like an assault on Vi's senses, and she wanted to shake the woman.

Motive, Violet thought, think of their motives. Fanny had been trying to rid herself of Lyle, seeking to end his pursuit. For Michael—his motive for killing his best friend was sheer, unadulterated fury for Lyle's pursuit of Fanny. Perhaps Ricky or Gervais had fathered Pamela's baby? If one of them knew the child could be his and Lyle found out? Could Lyle have been murdered while confronting whichever it might be?

What about that argument in the woods where someone was going to be ruined? Surely it was all wrapped up together. Who could tell, however, with these friends? They probably tortured each other for sport.

Violet paused as another door opened and Gervais stepped into the hall, playing with the cuffs of his sleeves. He glanced between the friends. "What's all this?"

"Bit of a ruckus," Ricky said with a grin. He nodded his head towards the hole in the wall and then at Jovie holding the weeping Fanny. "Been exciting."

"Didn't think little Fanny would mourn Lyle like this." Gervais knew he was taunting Fanny, and she lifted her head to shoot him a watery, terrified glare.

Jovie snapped, "She isn't, you fool."

Fanny pushed away from Jovie and rushed into her room, slamming the door behind her.

"Dramatic." Gervais sounded almost amused.

Violet hadn't liked him before, but at that moment? She'd have happily kneed him in the delicate area and shoved him down a short flight of stairs. Not enough to do anything more than bruise him, but she wanted him to be bruised enough for it to ache for days.

"I suggest that you close your mouth and think." Violet snapped her mouth closed as well. They needed the dramatic revelations to trap the killer sooner, but she was just so angry.

"Think about what, my *lady?*" Gervais demanded. "I didn't do anything wrong."

"You were in the process of being ruined. Isn't that what I heard?" She was *nearly* certain that Gervais had been there. She had seen him furiously storming off afterwards. "Maybe that's why you killed Lyle?"

"Me?" Gervais laughed. "I would have been fine eventually. A bit of setback. Nothing more."

"Is that why you've been haunting my steps more than normal this time?" Jovie asked. "Michael told you of the money from my parents, didn't he? My aunt and uncle won't let me have it until I marry. You thought you could marry me and have it? No."

"No? You think you haven't been mine for the taking this whole time?"

Jovie's gaze narrowed. She took a deep breath in as she bit back what had to be a rabid diatribe. She cursed and then spun, running down the stairs. Vi glanced at Ham and whispered, "Gervais and Ricky are the likeliest to have fathered Pamela's baby. Did you hear of the argument in the wood?"

He nodded. "Do you think Lyle was forcing himself on Fanny?"

Vi winced, but she shook her head. "I don't think she'd have been able to be around him. Not if he was hurting her like that regularly. They were telling jokes on the train. Fanny wasn't even uncomfortable."

"Lyle is something of a wartish fiend," Gervais admitted, "but he wouldn't go that far. Besides, he wanted to steal her back from Michael not make her hate him."

"Vi," Hamilton said just as softly, giving Gervais a commanding look when he seemed to lean in. Gervais backed up. "Women endure horrible things and somehow seem to keep on acting as though nothing is wrong."

Vi shook her head all the same. "I just don't think so. I don't think she's that good of an actress."

Hamilton paused and then nodded. "I trust your instincts, Vi. Michael, however, is killing mad."

"You don't have to be angry to murder."

"But one often is," Hamilton said, grinning when she tossed him an exasperated look. "Get Jovie. Stay with her. She can't trust her friends, not even that cousin of hers. Any of them could have killed Lyle, and Michael is the obvious suspect."

"If only there were evidence—"

CHAPTER 12

*J*ovie hadn't been stupid enough to go off alone. She was pacing the large hunting lodge's foyer, bypassing the lush oversized seats. And, Vi hoped, avoiding the gazes of the many dead animals lining the walls.

Vi was tempted to applaud Jovie for not rushing off too far. Instead, she walked up to the front desk and requested an automobile and information. The man raised his brows and said, "It'll take a few minutes."

"Of course it will," Vi answered. "Take your time." She requested a pen and paper and left a note for Jack while they waited for the auto to arrive.

"What's all this?" Jovie asked when Violet approached with a, "Shall we?"

"Your friends aren't ready for our interfering, so we're off to cause the good kind of trouble."

"Is there a good kind?"

Vi didn't answer, and they waited quietly for the auto.

"Tell me about Fanny before Lyle and Michael," Violet said as they took the backseat of the auto. She handed the driver the card with the address. "What was she like when you were little?"

"Quiet. Pamela was always the star among us. The bright one."

"Yet everyone loves Fanny now."

"Well, we grew up, didn't we?" Jovie gestured with her hands to her chest. "She didn't just end up with the better figure, she was nicer. I always thought Lyle wanted the one who was hardest to get. Fanny didn't give her heart easily."

"So if she'd just given into him once, he'd have let her go?"

"He'd probably have told Michael and ruined Fanny's life."

"Oh, he was a peach. What do you know about their investments together?"

"They all invested in a brewery."

"A brewery?" Violet laughed. It wasn't a terrible plan. People would drink alcohol when there wasn't money for anything else. A good pint, fish and chips, it was the English way. If the beer were decent enough, they might make good money.

"*All* of them?"

"I think so," Jovie said. "They were all sort of excited for a while. When things get rough, they all stress."

"They are making some poor talented brew..." Vi's head tilted as considered. "What do you call a brew person? Brew bloke? Brewer? I—"

Jovie shrugged.

"Whatever you call the person. The one with the real

skills. They're making the poor man crazy, I bet. I can just imagine the fellow going home and telling his wife all about those rich blokes who think they know so much."

Jovie laughed. "Lyle is"—she paused and her eyes filled with tears again—"was. He was controlling. I never thought about the poor man whose business was invested in. He probably does hate them."

"Not as much as he will when they all pull their funds out of his business and ruin everything he worked for." Violet reminded herself to look into who the poor man was and see what could be done.

"Why do you think about the man on the other end of the business?"

"I've invested in a few businesses," Violet said. The auto turned up a curving road and Violet hopped out before the driver could open her door. "I'm excited! I've never got to do this end of things."

Jovie ran her hand through her hair. "What are we doing? Why are there children playing outside? I—"

"Mischief! The good kind. Come on!"

"Mrs. Wakefield?" one of the children called. "Mama said to bring you inside. Are you gonna be nice to them?"

"Yes!" Violet crossed her finger over her chest. "The snuggles will be endless. They'll be so very spoiled."

"Snuggles?"

Violet glanced back at Jovie and grinned. She winked and then the boy opened the door to the yips of puppies. "Puppies!"

"Puppies?" Jovie gasped. "Puppies!"

There was a box in the corner, and Violet knelt next to it. "Oh my goodness! Look at all the sweet little slobber. They're going to get dog spit over everything Ham owns."

Jovie laughed and Violet glanced up at her. "Dogs make everything better. You should get one. They look at you with those pretty, large eyes and think you're the best thing they've ever seen or known."

Violet lifted one of the bulldog puppies and pressed its cheeks together. "Look at these eyes!"

"He's pretty cute."

"He?" Violet asked, frowning. "I need both a Watson and a Mary."

"Both? What if he doesn't want two?"

Vi grinned. "Then Jack and I will have four dogs instead of two. Are they ready to go?"

The woman who was watching them from the doorway nodded. "If you're going to get two, you should get ones from different litters that aren't related."

Vi's mouth twisted. "I really wanted to torment my friend with two dogs today."

"The other's not far."

Vi grinned evilly. "Perfect!"

VIOLET WALKED BACK up the hotel steps only to see Jack and Hamilton step onto the large wrap around porch when she did. She had a puppy in her arms and Jovie was a step behind with the second.

"I guess they were safe," Ham told Jack, whose jaw was clenching.

"I left a note, and I stayed with Jovie like you asked." Violet eyed him, taking in the look of relief combined with furious anger.

"Our rooms were destroyed," Jack said. "The note with

the room. It took me hours to realize that you had left with Jovie."

Violet started to reply and then handed Jack the puppy. She jerked her head at Jovie, who thrust the second puppy at Hamilton. When they were both bound by wriggling little dogs, Violet said, "We couldn't have possibly known that our rooms were going to be destroyed." She felt surprisingly unconcerned about it with puppies to snuggle.

Jack eyed her, his gaze running over her body. "I suppose you're all right."

"We got to play with puppies," Violet said a shrug. She darted in and cupped his cheek. "I'm fine. I'm sorry you were worried."

Jack shifted the pup to one arm and pulled her by her neck towards him to press his forehead against hers. "I didn't like that feeling."

Violet nodded against him and whispered, "We wanted to cause good mischief."

"You did," Hamilton said. The puppy was licking his chin frantically.

"That's Mary. I knew you'd like her best."

"Is this Watson?" Jack demanded, scratching the ears of the other one.

"You'll like him best. Rouge and I know you prefer Holmes. You're breaking Rouge's heart."

Jack wrapped his arm around Violet's waist. "We've been moved into a suite with multiple rooms. We have you moved with us, Jovie. Along with Lila and Denny, so we can all look after each other."

A terrible thought occurred to Violet. "What happened to my clothes?"

"Good news, Vi," Hamilton told her gently. "You get to go shopping."

Violet gasped, holding her hand to her heart. "This is not fair. I already had to do this once, and Lila and I are *not* the same size. How did they get into our room?"

"Housekeeping is missing their keys. Apparently, they've been gone for a few days."

Violet groaned. "But I love my clothes." She stopped following Jack as what that might mean occurred to her. "Does that...does it have anything to do with your case?"

"Maybe?" Jack told her. "We don't know what it means. Ham's rooms were rifled, and they took both his notebooks and the pound notes on his bedside table."

She turned towards him on the lift. "It *could* mean that his death was planned. If the housekeeping keys have anything to do with the murder."

"It seemed very spur of the moment," Jack told her. "Given what we know about how he died."

Violet stared at him. "What? Did someone hit him with a stick or something?"

Hamilton shook his head as Jack closed his eyes. "Your wife is too smart."

"She's right?" Jovie demanded. "*Bloody hell.*"

Violet groaned. "Life is not fair. I did not want to imagine that." She paused, pressing her fingers to her temples. "Someone could have wanted the murder to look spur of the moment."

"So someone got Lyle to join them in the garden and then hit him with a stick? Surely that rules out Fanny and Pamela?"

Jack and Hamilton hesitated long enough for Violet to sigh.

"Clearly not."

"How do you know?" Jovie asked. "Why would you think that it doesn't leave them out? Don't you think you'd have to be very strong in order to murder someone that way?"

"Don't ask that," Vi hissed. "We'll have details I do *not* want to have! Do *any* of them have alibis?"

"Ricky was with a lady friend."

"He doesn't have lady friends here," Jovie said.

Violet lifted a brow.

"It wasn't me!"

"A paid lady friend?" Violet asked.

"Ew!" Jovie answered.

The lift stopped on a new floor and Jack led the way to a set of rooms that had a double door. There was a police constable outside, and he opened the door as they approached.

"Oh wow," Jovie breathed.

Violet glanced around and then demanded, "Why didn't we rent these rooms the first time?"

CHAPTER 13

*P*amela Craft did not answer her bedroom door, but Fanny Browne did. She took a look at Jovie and then demanded, "What is *happening*? Do they really think that one of us killed Lyle? Surely it was a tramp."

"I don't know," Jovie lied, reaching out and taking Fanny's hand. "What *has been* happening?"

Fanny put her hand over her mouth and shook her head. Tears immediately swam in her eyes and Violet resisted an urge to slap the woman silly. Was *this* the woman that the friends had both adored? That one friend had seemingly betrayed another for? Men who were supposedly as close as brothers?

"Fan." Jovie took her hand gently. "Fanny, you have to tell us."

"Why? Why do I have to go over it again and again?"

Jovie squeezed Fanny's hand, then crossed to the chairs

near the small table. "You have to tell us," Jovie said, "because you and Michael are suspects in Lyle's murder."

Fanny gasped and started babbling, but Vi ignored it. The usual reaction and Violet felt certain that she'd seen it too many times to care. To distract herself, Vi glanced around the room. Everything was in place. Fanny had been sitting by the window with a book before they arrived, but Violet saw the bookmark was on the first few pages. How long had Fanny been sitting alone, pretending to read, while her husband was off doing who knew what? Why was she acting like she was the one who had been committing crimes?

"It's not your fault," Violet told Fanny, cutting through Fanny's harsh, self-hating whispering.

"But..."

"It's not your fault," Violet said again. "Nothing about this is your fault."

"I should have told Michael."

Violet's gaze narrowed and fury rode her so hard that she wanted to scream. Instead, she said in a low, gritty voice, "He should have been a safe person for you to tell."

Jovie stared at Violet as Fanny sniffled.

"It's not his fault."

"It's not your fault," Violet repeated. "Did you flirt with Lyle when Michael wasn't around?"

Fanny shook her head frantically.

"Did you promise Lyle to always love him and never love another?"

Fanny shook her head again. "He said we were moving too fast, and we should reconsider. We were young. Maybe too young to decide who to be with for the rest of our lives. I cried for weeks, and then I went home with Jovie, and Michael was there. He's so kind."

Violet's mouth twisted. She wanted to shake Fanny except Vi had seen the couple together. She'd seen their broken-hearted whispering. Vi was sure, utterly sure, that Michael Browne loved his wife.

"Why are you acting guilty? Did you kill Lyle Craft?"

Fanny paused long enough for Violet to think that maybe Fanny had. Only, no. There was no way that Fanny Browne would leave the side of her then-aware husband to join Lyle on the grounds. "Michael wasn't with you, was he?"

Fanny's eyes widened. "Of course he was."

"Oh my goodness," Jovie huffed. "She's lying. Look at her face. She always flushes like that and avoids your gaze when she's lying. It's why she rarely tries."

"Jovie!" Fanny cried.

Jovie was staring at Fanny. "You think Michael killed Lyle."

Fanny started to answer and then looked away.

"Oh my goodness," Jovie repeated, sitting down. "I didn't think it would be them."

"It isn't us," Fanny cried. "Neither of us would kill anyone."

"Are you afraid?" Vi examined Fanny's face looking for some sign that she needed help.

"Of Michael? Of course not."

Violet glanced at Jovie, checking for a lie, but she shook her head.

"But Michael wasn't with you the night Lyle died?"

Fanny refused to speak. She just shook her head, but the crying started again.

"Oh, for the love of all that is holy!" Violet shouted, standing up. "Lying doesn't help anyone, Fanny. Either your husband killed Lyle—and if so, Michael *will* be caught—or he didn't and your lying is only distracting the detectives from finding the real killer."

"You aren't a detective," Fanny shot back.

Vi laughed. "Too true. I'm sure they'll be around soon. Again. They'll be interested in knowing why you were lying about Michael being with you. And, of course, someone probably saw him, so your lie will trap him deeper into the role of killer even if he isn't."

Fanny paused then and something that proclaimed her more than a weeping willow flowed over her face. "Michael did not kill Lyle."

"Why?"

"He loved him," Fanny snapped.

"Even after Michael found out whatever Lyle was doing to you?"

"He wasn't hurting me. Michael read more into it than he should have. Lyle was...too attentive. Too touchy. Too likely to follow me and compliment me and touch my hair and get too close, but he didn't *hurt* me."

"So how did Michael find out about what Lyle was doing?"

Fanny bit her lip. "I found out I was expecting. He was so excited. Lyle's child and our child would be like siblings. And I...I told him everything. I didn't want our baby anywhere near Lyle. I don't like Pamela. I haven't for a long time."

Violet stared as her mind flipped ahead. "Did Michael say what he was going to do?"

"He said he'd take care of it. That he'd end things and it would all be over."

"And then?" Jovie stood.

"And then Lyle turned up dead," Violet answered for Fanny. "Fanny thinks Michael might have killed Lyle. It's why she's lying about what happened."

Jovie closed her eyes. "But…"

"He didn't."

"Lyle didn't rape you."

Fanny shook her head.

"He scared you. He was aggressive?"

"Michael made me answer the door to our room as if I was alone. It was Lyle. The moment Lyle thought Michael wasn't there, he changed. Michael saw it all. He was so angry. He shoved Lyle out of our room, and Michael and I talked for hours. I told him everything."

Violet thought back. She'd seen them whispering in the massage room. Then, she'd gone back to Jack and slept. They'd woken late and went swimming. Somewhere in there, Lyle had been killed. If Michael had discovered the truth, he might have been the one who murdered Lyle.

"Did Michael discover the truth the day he followed you into the massage rooms?"

Fanny stared at Violet. "You knew about that?"

Violet nodded.

"I told him after we arrived here. He promised me he would separate our lives, but he kept bringing it up every moment we were alone. *Was* I sure? I finally got so angry I told him I'd prove it. It was before I went to the baths that Lyle came to our door. When Michael saw how Lyle was around me, when he got so angry, I ran. I left them together, *but* I saw Lyle alive after that. We all did at dinner."

Violet rose and began to pace. "The motives are these: Fanny, she killed Lyle to finally be rid of him."

Fanny gasped, but Violet ignored it. She hardly cared if Fanny was offended. Violet knew already they'd never be friends. She could hardly stand the woman as it was.

"Any of the men who had invested with Michael and Lyle also have a motive. I assume it was both Ricky and Gervais?"

Fanny nodded, gaze wide.

"Michael told them it was over? That he was done?"

Fanny nodded again. "We needed the money to start a real household, and once Michael promised me to let us live separately from them—he would have told the others. He said we'd take a loss, but it wouldn't ruin us."

"It was going to ruin someone," Violet muttered. "People kill over that all the time. Do you know which one might have done so?"

Fanny shook her head. Vi glanced at Jovie, but she shook her head too.

"Ricky has an alibi, so even if it was Ricky…"

"No," Jovie told Vi. "He doesn't have a lot of money right now, but his parents are quite wealthy. Sooner or later, he'll be fine. He's an only child."

Violet paced, fiddling with her wedding ring. "He was always the least likely given the alibi. A paid companion isn't going to lie to the constables for someone they don't love." Violet tilted her head. "Gervais, if he was the one who would be ruined, might have done so. Pamela if Lyle realized he'd been manipulated into marriage. How did she do that?"

Jovie answered. "Appearances matter to him. He wouldn't have been able to father a baby on one of our friends and abandon it. He believed he had to marry her."

"Pamela, Gervais, Fanny, and Michael."

Violet glanced behind her at the longtime friends. "I need to talk to Hamilton and Jack."

Jovie rose slowly to follow Violet.

"You're leaving me?" Fanny demanded.

"I promised Jack that Violet wouldn't be alone."

"So you're going to leave me alone?" Fanny demanded. "We're family."

"You can come with us," Violet offered and Fanny stepped back as though she'd said something terribly insulting.

"You should stay here with me," Fanny told Jovie. "How can you even think of doing anything else?"

Jovie's wicked expression had faded and all that was left was a wincing apology. "It's not safe."

"You mean I'm not safe. You surely don't think that we'd hurt you."

Jovie looked at Violet for help. It wasn't a question that Violet could answer for her.

Carefully, Jovie spoke. "Lyle thought he was safe with whoever killed him, Fanny. I don't want to hurt you, but I also don't want to die. I'm not going to risk my life on the hope that you and Michael are who I want you to be."

Fanny stepped back, her hand to her chest. "Will you throw away everything that we have?"

"You think I don't know that I'm the unwanted niece that Michael's parents didn't want?"

Fanny gaped. "You know I don't feel that way about you."

Jovie's expression didn't seem to agree fully, but she only said, "If you think it's possible that Michael might have killed Lyle, then I need to as well."

Fanny was left speechless and weeping as they left. Violet crossed to Pamela Craft's door again and knocked. When she didn't answer, Vi tried the door. To her surprise, it wasn't locked, and she peeked inside. "Hello?"

CHAPTER 14

"*P*ammy left," Gervais said with a grin.

Jack had just stepped into the hall, so Violet only lifted a brow.

"Pammy?" Jack asked from behind Gervais, making him squeak as he turned. "I've had a rather interesting conversation with Michael Browne."

"The one where he says I killed Lyle instead of him?" Gervais's laugh was mocking. "Jovie darling, surely you don't think such things of me?"

"Where were you when Lyle was murdered?"

"I don't know when that was." Gervais's smile was smarmy indeed. Violet stepped back to watch as Jack questioned Gervais, shooting question after question at him. Every time Jack asked a question, Gervais gave a possibly true answer with a mocking grin. He was so mocking that Violet was tempted to box his ears.

"Do you know what happens when you lie during an investigation?"

Gervais laughed. "Who says I'm lying?"

"I do," Violet finally said. "Bloody hell, Jack, let's just let Hamilton arrest them all and wait for them to turn on each other."

Jack glanced at Violet, and she saw a gleam of interest in his gaze.

"Did you beat Lyle Craft to death?" Violet demanded from Gervais.

He stepped into Violet's space and reached up to tug a hair, but Jack grabbed Gervais's wrist. "Careful."

Gervais held up his free hand in surrender. "I just wanted to see what you'd do. That's the telling part there, my friend. You'd murder me for hurting your wife."

Jack's gaze narrowed. "I would."

"You're not the only man who feels that way," Gervais said, twisting his arm from Jack's grip and stepping back. "Just making a point."

Violet watched Gervais walk away with a deep scowl. "It's very likely that Michael Browne *did* kill Lyle Craft."

Jack didn't look convinced, which made Violet reconsider. Only, there was no evidence. There was no evidence for any of them.

"He got beaten to death?" Violet asked.

Jovie squeaked, but she bit back any further reaction.

"Let's go back to our rooms, Vi."

Violet followed Jack with Jovie at her side. He hurried, bypassing the hunting lodge's manager who tried to get his attention. People looked up as they passed and their eyes trailed after Jack. "You're famous now."

"I've talked to a lot of people trying to find a witness."

"Nothing?" she asked as the constable outside of the suite opened the door for them.

"Nothing," Jack said. "Like you guessed, Lyle was killed with a heavy branch. There are no prints. The ground there was thick grass, and it didn't show anything. No bloody clothes have been discovered. We've searched rooms. No one has an alibi except Ricky. There's no evidence at all."

"What about in our rooms?"

Jack shook his head again.

Violet groaned and then looked up as the door to the bedroom that Denny and Lila had taken opened.

"What's all this? Slumming with us non-detectives?" Denny asked. "Get over it already, Vi. Demand chalkboards. Pull in the suspects with the evidence of their crimes behind them and pick a fight."

"I don't want to take notes," Lila said. "I got chalk all over my black dress the last time I did and I can't seem to shake the scent."

"Darling," Denny declared, "that's in your imagination."

"You've made an interesting point," Jack said as Hamilton also entered the suite.

"Did we discover something?"

"Your dogs ate Lila's shoe," Denny said. "Violet adopted devil dogs."

"They're sweet," Violet gasped. "Angels."

"Oh, we like them. Can we have the devil female?"

"Yes," Hamilton answered as Violet said, "No!"

"Is that the interesting point?" Violet asked Jack, frowning at Ham and Denny.

"It's hot," Jack told them. "We're irritable and we like each other. None of your friends trust each other, Jovie."

"She's aware," Violet said.

Jovie frowned and nodded. "I ruined my relationship

with Fanny today. She was one of my two favorite people and when it came right down to it, I realized I didn't trust her with my life."

"Ouch," Denny said. "We're all you have and I have to say—that's too bad. We're cursed."

"People like us are spoiled," Violet told Denny. "Spoiled, self-righteous prigs who don't see the people around them as real souls with depths in their hearts that reach untold levels."

"What?" Denny gaped.

"Think about it. These friends are breaking with each other and in so doing, they'll ruin whoever started that brewery they all invested in. Their fight is more important than the man who built the business. That person isn't real to them."

Jack stared. His penetrating gaze was fixed on Violet and he was watching her as she paced around the suite.

"It's like your cousin, Jack. He poisoned those pistachios and sent them to a home of a widowed mother, putting every person in reach of her chocolates at risk."

"I don't understand," Jovie said.

"They call us bright young things, but for the most part, we bring darkness and pain. We aren't cursed, we just associate with people who've lost perspective and feeling. The idea of honor is long since gone from our people and all that is left is expectation that we deserve something that we haven't worked for."

"If you were to put us in a hot room," Jack asked, "and poke at our friendships and loyalties, what would happen?"

Denny glanced at Violet and Lila and then said, "Lila would probably nap."

"Violet would poke back." Lila yawned.

"But my friends wouldn't," Jovie answered. "You put us in a hot room and start churning up our secrets? We'd turn on each other."

"Exactly," Jack said. "We don't have any evidence. The only one I trust to not be lying to me is you, Jovie."

Her laugh was hollow in reply to that.

Hamilton reach down to pick up one of his puppies. "You want to pull one of Vi's tricks? Try to get them to turn on each other? We need to have a theory first. Something more than just the knowledge that *one* of them is the killer."

Violet paced past the others. "We could always lie."

"That could turn on us easily, Vi."

She glanced back. "Let's be real here. Fanny didn't do it."

"Why not?" Jovie asked.

"Because she wouldn't have followed Lyle outside. And Michael believed her. She didn't need to get rid of him."

"Ricky has an alibi," Ham added. "He's a real piece of work. I do *not* care for any of them."

"So we're left with Gervais and Michael," Jack said.

"Oh no," Lila said lazily. "Pamela Craft is definitely a suspect. She has mean eyes."

Jack and Ham frowned. "She's very...ah...with child."

"Do you remember Kate?" Vi asked.

"She was sick quite a bit and her ankles were very disturbing, so yes. I will always remember them."

"She went mad," Violet told him, rolling her eyes. "Kate! Sweet, kind, mild Kate. With child? Kate was terrifying, and we *like* her."

"Ah," Hamilton said, looking at Jack. They both

winced, not wanting to admit that even they found Kate alarming.

"So, what if Pamela—who is significantly less kind than Kate—finally realizes that her husband will never love her. She'll never be anything other than ignored, even bearing his child?"

Jovie hesitated and then said, "No one is convinced that Lyle is the father."

"What if Lyle was starting to realize he wasn't the father?"

"Well, if pregnant Kate was afraid of her husband, she would have stabbed Victor in his sleep and then slept next to his bleeding body."

"Oh," Jovie gasped.

"Lila's been a little more terrifying than usual lately," Denny agreed. "I'm with Vi. A pregnant woman assuming she *could* kill him physically? On top of everything else? Certainly."

Jack and Ham glanced at each other and Ham was smiling as he shook his head, but he said, "So we include Pamela Craft on the suspect list."

"Pamela has a strong motive. Michael an even stronger one. Gervais's is good enough."

"So we gather them up, make them uncomfortable, and pick a fight," Denny told them gleefully.

Hamilton glanced among the friends. "It can't hurt. Eventually we'll find evidence if this doesn't work."

"It'll work better if you get Jovie to help."

Jovie stared, horrified as she realized what they were asking her to do. "I need to think."

VIOLET FOLLOWED Jack into their bedroom. The thick of the afternoon was on them and the heat was heavy in the air. Violet sat down and peeled off her stockings as she watched Jack remove his jacket.

"Do you think it'll work?"

Jack shrugged. "It might."

Violet crossed to their bed, flopped onto it, and gazed up at the ceiling. She closed her eyes against the heat and considered. "Who do you think did it?"

Jack lay down next to her, tangling their fingers together. "I can see why Michael Browne would have killed Lyle. When this started, I couldn't imagine killing Ham or Denny. I know they wouldn't do to you what Lyle did to Fanny, but if they did? I'd have to try very hard to not kill someone over that."

Violet turned onto her side, propping her head up on her hand. "What if I forced you to marry me by pretending to carry a baby that wasn't yours?"

Jack huffed a surprised laugh and then kissed her on the forehead. "That scenario only works if I hadn't wanted you before. I've wanted you since I first saw you."

Violet rolled her eyes. She ignored the heat to lay her head down on Jack's arm. "You did not."

"You were on the train with your brother. Joking about that stupid bet book. You noticed that we heard you, and you felt a flash of shame. Your mouth twisted and I thought you had lovely lips. Later, you helped poor Gwennie when she was sicking-up, and you threw yourself at your aunt. I knew you didn't kill her even though my professionalism required evidence. You were too happy to see her."

Violet's mouth pinched at the familiar pain. "I told

Jovie about how I miss her. The pain doesn't go away. I have thought since the twins were born that when I have a baby, she won't be there to hold her. It makes losing Aunt Agatha fresh all over again."

Jack pulled Violet in and whispered into her hair. "Just because you won't see her doesn't mean she won't be there."

"Looking over me from heaven?"

"Certainly."

Violet closed her eyes, letting him hold her close while she considered the fairytale. Was it possible? Perhaps having found a love like Jack's she should consider nothing less, but she wasn't sure she did. There was so much pain in living. And in loving.

In this breathtakingly beautiful hotel crossed with a hunting lodge, someone had been betrayed so deeply that they'd killed one of the people who they should have loved best. It happened over and over again. And over and over again, Violet was surprised at the cruelty and capacity for hatred that mankind held within them.

"How do we believe in something beautiful when things are so dark?"

Jack didn't answer for so long that Violet wasn't sure he was still awake. She sat up, examining his face, and found his gaze fixed on her. "Violet, surely in a world with so much love there has to be a corresponding depth of hatred?"

"What love?"

"Ours for each other, for the twins, Victor's for you and yours for Victor. Your Aunt Agatha's. All of our friends. I know things are dark. By Jove, how could they not be? We need to focus on the good."

Violet shook her head, but she wasn't feeling dark. She was feeling something else. Something resolved.

"Or," Violet offered, "we create the good. We decide right now to do better."

Jack's gaze roved over her face. "Or," he agreed, "we create the good. How do you want to do that?"

Violet laid her head back down. "I thought we might start by catching a killer and then help the poor brewer these people are probably going to ruin."

"And then?"

"Whatever else strikes our fancy."

CHAPTER 15

*J*ack walked into the room the hunting lodge had provided and looked at Violet.

"What have you done?"

Violet bit down on her bottom lip to hide an evil grin. "Who me?"

"Bloody hell, Vi. It's like Hades in here. What did you do?"

"I had the servants light a fire and close the windows for the last few hours."

Jack stared at Violet with an edge of humor twitching along his lips. "We're going to be in here too. It's like the inside of an oven."

"We'll be fine." Violet crossed to him and kissed his chin. "Be strong, love."

His gaze moved over her and he knew her well enough to ask, "What else have you done?"

"Me?"

"Violet," Jack said sternly, but it had little effect.

She grinned at him, letting the mischief fill her eyes.

His gaze narrowed. "*What* else did you do?"

Vi confessed. "I might have paid their waiter to charge their wine to our rooms and top off regularly. Possibly I sent an 'apology' round of cocktails from the management to the table as well."

"So you pushed them into their cups. We need a confession, not drunken blubbering."

Vi shrugged. They intended to pick a fight between the friends and see what came out. The chances of a confession were low. The chances of discovering more secrets? That was much higher. The chances of discovering those secrets when someone was uncomfortable, a little zozzled, and you were prodding them? Much, much higher.

"This is morally shaky ground, don't you think?"

Vi shook her head. "It's not like we're going to publish the secrets they reveal unless they contributed to the murder. We won't even repeat them. I don't care. You don't. Lila and Denny will probably forget by tomorrow and Hamilton has actual morals that will keep him from judging them or repeating their stories. Jovie's friends will only be a cautionary tale among our friends and everything else will continue to be kept private."

Jack frowned and then glanced around the room before seeing the drinks table. "Is that only cocktails?"

Violet nodded and then considered. "There are chocolate liqueurs as well."

"You already mixed the drinks?"

Vi nodded.

"Particularly strong?"

Vi attempted an innocent look and was saved when the door to the room opened.

"Oh my," Denny moaned. He pressed his hand to his chest as he stepped farther into the room. "Have I stepped onto the face of the sun? What has happened?"

"Violet," Jack said, taking a piece of dripping ice from the ice bucket and popping it into his mouth.

"Oh," Denny groaned. "She really is a pretty devil."

"Probably you should reconsider that drink," Violet told Denny as he sipped it and then gasped at the burn.

"I'm just here for the show, Vi." Denny sipped the drink again. "I'm not going to help. Other than to, you know, say something snide or laugh."

Lila and Hamilton joined them. Lila gasped and then took the heavily iced drink that Denny handed her while Ham glanced at Jack and asked, "Vi?"

Jack nodded. "She's been sending them drinks as well."

"Oh, Vi." Ham ran his hand over his jaw. "We should have known she would."

"Mmmm," Jack agreed.

There was a knock a moment later. A constable brought Pamela Craft into the room with her hand on her swollen belly. She gasped at the heat. "What happened here?"

The fire had been out for long enough to hide it had existed at all.

"There seems to be a bit of a malfunction in the heating," Jack lied. "Unfortunately, the hunting lodge isn't able to provide another room."

Denny stepped forward, winking at Vi and said, "This will help." He pressed a drink into Pamela's hand and showed her to a seat. A moment later, the door opened again with another constable and the Browne couple.

Michael and Fanny walked into the room with pale

skin, dark circles under their eyes, and gazes that carefully missed everyone else's. It was Lila who handed them both drinks. Before they were even seated, Gervais, Ricky, and Jovie arrived.

"By Jove, has someone turned on the heat in here?" Gervais demanded. He loosened his tie immediately and took his own drink to the window. He tried to open it, but Violet had paid the hotel to nail them shut. "Why don't the windows open?"

"Apparently the man who was fixing them misunderstood his directions." Violet's lie didn't pass muster for Gervais, who snorted. He took a large drink from his glass and lifted a brow at Violet.

"Perhaps we'll begin with a timeline," Ham told them once everyone was situated in the sweltering room.

"Of what?" Ricky demanded. "I have an alibi. Why do I have to be here?"

"Maybe because you might know something?" Jovie's sarcasm was a bit more vicious than Vi would have expected of her, but they had told Jovie to pick fights.

"Know what? Who wanted to kill Lyle?"

"Yes," Jovie snapped. "Clearly."

"Well, I don't." Ricky set his drink aside. "I don't have to stand for this."

"Sit down, Mr. Hemming," Hamilton told him. "You're all under suspicion of murder. You all have motives."

"But whose motive is greater than Michael's?" Gervais asked with a bit of a smirk.

"Let's return to the timeline," Hamilton repeated calmly.

"Make sure you start at the right place then," Gervais said. "Back when we were in school and Lyle pursued

BETH BYERS

Fanny because she wasn't interested in him. Did he ever really want her or did he just want her to want him? It's a question I've debated for years."

Violet held back her shout of triumph. She had known they would turn on each other if they were prodded properly. The murder had already destroyed them. They just hadn't realized it yet.

Then again, Gervais seemed the sort happy to air the dirty linen in public.

"How can you say that?" Fanny pressed her fingers to her lips.

"Do stop with the weeping. You aren't prettier crying like Pamela. No one wants to see your act."

Pamela gasped and then pressed her hand to her baby again.

"Do not talk to my wife like that," Michael warned Gervais.

"You don't get to tell me what to do anymore," Gervais snapped back. "You ruined our business venture and probably poor Harry King's life."

"Is he the brewer?" Vi regretted stepping in when they were turning on each other so nicely, but she was shocked that Gervais thought of anyone but himself that she forgot herself.

Gervais nodded as Michael said, "Did you know that Lyle was harassing Fanny?"

"Everyone knew," Gervais told Michael flatly. "Why didn't you?"

Michael jerked as though he'd been punched in the stomach and he looked down.

"You decided to ruin us all in order to get revenge on Lyle for pursuing Fanny after you married her, but you were the only one who didn't see what was happening. How were we supposed to know you didn't know when it was so *obvious?*"

Michael mopped his brow. "Can't we open the door?"

"I assumed that you all hoped to keep your privacy," Ham answered, "but if you don't mind rumors and half-truths spreading about you, we can. I'm sure the press will be here soon. They'll be very interested in what you have to say."

"Back to the timeline," Violet said when no one agreed to Michael's suggestion. "In your school days, Fanny was linked to Lyle. Who was Michael linked to? Pamela?"

"Pamela was chasing after a rich banker's son then," Ricky said with a snort. "Of course, she always had eyes for old Lyle. He was a handsome enough lad in those days."

Violet glanced between the friends. Pamela had her hand on her baby, rubbing in circles, but her eyes weren't filled with grief. They were filled with fury. She did seem to hate Gervais, but it extended to Fanny as well.

"Did you know that your husband wanted Fanny?" Violet asked Pamela. "Here you are growing his baby, and he's pursuing his best friend's wife."

Gervais and Ricky snorted, but Pamela shot them a silent, killing look.

"He was no best friend," Michael inserted. "He was a demon."

Vi tried shooting him a quelling look, but it didn't work.

Pamela put on a sorrowful look. "This is hard for me and the baby. Orphaned before he was born. It's too hard. Too, too hard."

Jovie jerked and then said something Vi knew she'd have kept back if possible. "But is the baby orphaned? Surely there's only a slight chance that Lyle was actually the baby's father."

Pamela gasped and then she put her hand to her face as she moaned. "How can you say such a thing?"

"Perhaps because Ricky and I have been enjoying your bed since our school days," Gervais answered idly. "As easy as you are, you'd have thought that Lyle would have taken a chance with you. You had to get him drunk and then lie to get him to look your way after the banker's son married someone with money and connections."

"You bastard!"

"Is the baby mine?" Gervais demanded. "Or were you sleeping with the cricket team as well?"

Even Violet gasped at that one and Pamela looked around. "How can you let him talk to me like this?"

"You trapped Lyle into marriage, Pammy," Gervais told her after he took a huge drink from his cocktail glass. "Holy Hades, this room should turn you to repentance, Pamela. Take note of the feel of hell and imagine it'll be worse."

"You know what I think?" Jovie looked and sounded sick but her friends weren't paying attention to the emotion behind her words. "I think Lyle realized that Michael wasn't going to be persuaded back to friendship. I imagine you wouldn't have cared about that."

"Jovie, darling," Gervais said with a laugh, "I knew we were meant for each other."

Jovie shot him a disgusted expression. "Never. Think of me as your Fanny. Never am I going to want you." A musing expression crossed her face and she added wickedly, "I bet that was what Fanny told Lyle. Pamela, you finally got him to take you and then he continued wanting Fanny."

Pamela shot back as if the object of their argument wasn't sitting in the room. "Fanny isn't clever or talented or even that beautiful. The only reason he wanted her was because she didn't want him."

"Unlike you," Denny slid in, handing both Gervais and Pamela a second drink.

Gervais grinned. "Even this idiot saw that your husband didn't want you," he told Pamela.

"You know what's interesting," Violet said as she glanced around the room. "You all have such good reasons to kill Lyle."

CHAPTER 16

*P*amela was flushed. Sweat beaded on her brow and her upper lip. She wasn't unattractive on a normal day, but in these circumstances with the friends turning on each other, they were all pretty unattractive. Violet had little doubt her own sweat covered, flushed face wasn't her best look.

Michael had a dark look on his face, and he was holding Fanny's hand too hard. Vi winced at the painful expression Fanny was trying to hide.

Ricky, however, seemed to be dozing.

Vi looked pointedly at him until he opened his eyes. "Is the arguing so familiar that you can sleep through it?"

He snuffled and shrugged. "It wasn't me. You already know that. The rest of this is just window dressing. I'm not sure why we're putting up with this."

"Because," Jovie shot out before the idea to leave really settled, "Jack and Ham are Scotland Yard, and *we all* know it was one of us. Don't you care that you're sitting in a room with a friend who murdered another friend? Who's to say it won't be you next?"

Fanny squeaked and glanced about as though any of them might pull out a knife.

"I'm staying," Ricky countered, "because I know I didn't do it, and I'd like to know who did. Lyle was my friend. I care enough to help this *farce* along."

Violet's gaze switched to Gervais, who made a kissing look at her. There was a little something in his expression that declared the same feeling as Ricky. Or maybe, Violet thought, he didn't want to leave and *seem* like the killer to the others. Jack placed his hand on Gervais's shoulder after that smooching noise and squeezed. She was sure Jack didn't hurt Gervais, but the threat was implicit.

"You would have lost money," Vi said instead to Ricky, diving at a motive, any motive at all. "People kill for that all time." She turned to Fanny. "I am guessing it wasn't you."

Fanny's gaze darted to Michael and then she pressed her lips together. She looked guilty, Violet had to admit until you imagined her luring out Lyle and bashing him down.

"Michael is, of course," Vi continued, watching the married couple carefully, "a favorite suspect. He has so much motive. It's overwhelming. One could drown in all that motive."

Michael jerked, but he seemed unsurprised by the claim. "I didn't kill anyone."

"It must be hard for Michael to know even his wife suspects him," Violet said, watching. She glanced at Gervais and added, "Don't you think?"

"They'll get over it. They're disgustingly dependent on each other."

"So why are we all here? Find your evidence and arrest Michael," Pamela snapped. "It's too hot to linger. Of course it was Michael. He realized that his best friend was hurting his wife. He snapped and he killed Lyle."

Michael leaned forward and stared at Pamela and Violet couldn't help but watch her carefully. Was it too easy to guess that perhaps Pamela might have been the killer after all? And how to get someone like her to confess? Was she the one pointing fingers because she truly believed Michael killed her husband? Or was she the one pointing fingers at the obvious Michael because *she* killed her husband?

Violet stared at Pamela then at Gervais. He seemed to be calculating Pamela in his mind as well.

The woman met Violet's gaze in sheer fury. "It's unkind to play this out in front of me. Fanny even. Why are you torturing us? Just arrest Michael and be done with it."

Violet replied quietly. "Michael seems a little too dim to me."

Michael grunted.

"Pamela isn't," Fanny said desperately. "She is as clever as they come and conniving as well."

"Fanny love," Gervais laughed, "I wouldn't have thought it of you. Your Michael is a bit of a plodding old duck. And you *are right*. Pamela is no such thing. I see where you're going with this, and I like it. She's a much better villain."

"Don't talk about Michael like that," Fanny said. "This

is bad enough. Michael and Lyle were like brothers, and now he's gone, and we—at least—are mourning."

"Oh please, pet," Gervais told Fanny with too much glee. "None of us believe you are mourning Lyle. Only the death of your faith in Michael."

"It wasn't Michael!" Fanny said, still sounding just uncertain enough that her husband looked offended.

Violet held up her hand. "When exactly did you tell Michael about what was happening with Lyle?"

Fanny stumbled for a moment. "I asked him to break things off between Lyle and our family just after dinner that first day."

Violet glanced at Jack. "But you didn't tell him about all the details until just before you were in the bathing rooms?"

"I told him then, yes," Fanny admitted. She wasn't as stupid as Violet had initially thought. Quiet, yes. Pretty enough, certainly. Fanny had garnered Lyle's attention simply because she became Michael's wife.

"So what happened?" Violet asked.

"I couldn't explain exactly *why* I was bothered by Lyle at first because Michael was so angry. Then, Lyle came to our door and Michael stepped out of sight. When Lyle thought Michael wasn't there, he was very insinuating."

"That couldn't have gone well." Violet's gaze was fixed on Michael who looked resigned.

"M-m-michael stepped out from behind the door. They had words and a bit of—well, a bit of shoving, and I went to the baths."

"Fled," Gervais corrected, eyes alight with mischief. Jovie's hands were fisted. Her sick expression on her cousin.

"I *went* to the baths. Michael eventually followed me. We talked after that. He was still so angry, but he wasn't violent. He was just upset and...and...hurt."

"Where did you go?" Violet asked Michael. "That night? When you left Fanny?"

"She'd just told me the most terrible things. Things I'd witnessed. I know I shouldn't have left her, but I couldn't look at her."

"It wasn't her fault," Jovie muttered catching a black look from Michael.

"It was late," he continued, "Most of the staff weren't working."

That wasn't an answer. "But you knew it would be. You all did. You've been here so many times."

Michael rubbed his jaw as he admitted. "I knew it would be deserted. I wanted it to be. I could have time in the gymnasium. I could work out my frustration and figure out how to go on. I hadn't been thinking about hurting Lyle. Just...just breaking with him."

"Breaking the investment between all of us," Gervais said. "Taking out your anger on everyone who might have known."

"You should have told me," Michael roared.

"See!" Pamela cried, taking another drink. "See! That's what killed my poor Lyle."

"Did no one see you?" Violet asked gently as though she were on Michael's side. She wasn't, but the calculating glee that Pamela didn't hide well enough was not lost on Violet, Jack, or Ham.

"The gymnasium is on the main floor near the kitchens. It looks out at the back garden. I used the punching bag until very late. I heard the ruckus and the autos arriving. I saw the lanterns in the garden. I went back to my room when I saw that something was going on."

"Was Fanny there?"

He nodded.

"Was she bloody?"

"She was the same as when I left. The same pajamas, the same everything." He was fierce in his answer. "Fanny was there. She is too good and kind to have hurt Lyle. Even after everything. It was only our own child's arrival that brought out the protector in Fanny."

Violet stared at each of them, considering them in her head as she did and a telling point occurred to her. Whoever killed Lyle did not go out the front doors which were the only doors unlocked. They were unlocked *and* attended. Which meant that whoever went out and took care of Lyle had to have had the housekeeping key.

"So when was the housekeeping key stolen?" The question was for Ham. Were they utterly stupid, Violet wondered, to have not seen that connection before?

"I say, what?" Gervais asked.

Even Ricky sat up, no longer looking bored by the drama between the friends.

"Within hours of our arrival," Hamilton answered. "Mr. Halliburton believes it was taken from a housekeeping closet the staff was working out of just near their rooms."

"Did you know in that time frame that Michael intended to break your partnership?" Violet asked Gervais and Ricky. They both shook their heads. Really, Violet thought, they were all quite stupid.

Her gaze turned to Michael and Fanny. Violet had seen

them just after Michael had witnessed what happened with Lyle and Fanny. She had seen the tears in the husband's eyes, and they had *not* known that they were being observed.

"I suppose there could be both a thief and a killer," Violet said, though she didn't believe it. Not in these circumstances. Not when the key was necessary to exit the lodge unobserved.

Violet was suddenly sure of who had killed Lyle. She hadn't been sure before, but...the way the suspect had acted, the way she hadn't left. She had needed to throw suspicion on Michael, and it had worked. Violet had been half-convinced he was the killer when she'd entered the room. She didn't, however, believe it any longer.

"I say," Gervais said. "My rooms were rifled after that first day. I thought the maid had taken my cufflinks. The ruby ones I got from my Uncle Gervais. They were quite valuable."

"Did you make a complaint?" Ham demanded.

"How could I? When Lyle was dead? I was angry with him, but I wasn't going to distract from finding his killer."

"You fool," Violet told Gervais. "What were you thinking? That was important information."

"What does the housekeeping key have to do with the rest of this?" Gervais asked. "So someone used a key to get into our rooms. A thief isn't the same as a killer."

"True," Violet said, glancing at Hamilton. "Until you add in that the killer used a key to get out of the lodge unobserved. Why did they take your cufflinks? For the money perhaps? Why did they rifle our rooms? To throw us off the scent? To distract us? To discover what we knew so far? It *was* nothing."

"Why do you think that?" Jovie demanded. She leaned forward, curls bouncing around her face.

"No other room than ours had their things destroyed. Ham writes notes overtly in a black notebook." Truthfulness, Violet thought. Now time for a lie. She faced Pamela. "One of the maids saw you leave our rooms."

Pamela paled.

"She noted the pregnant belly. The dark circles. The maid thought you were looking for Jovie and didn't think anything of it until this morning."

"I—" Pamela stumbled.

"You were the only one who could have done it," Violet told Pamela. "No one else had the information that the key would be needed until after it was gone. You stole it just after we arrived, but *before* Gervais and Ricky realized that the partnership was going to break apart."

Pamela shook her head, but the tide of feeling turned on her in an instant, and she was trapped by her own choices. Not just from the last few days, but from every choice she'd made over the course of her friendship with these people.

CHAPTER 17

"No. You're wrong." Pamela placed her hand on her belly and rubbed it as if to say, 'Look at me. I'm a mother. I'd never commit a crime.' If only that were true, Violet thought, as Pamela wailed, "Of course you're wrong."

Violet's voice was almost gentle and kind as she told Pamela. "I saw Michael after he had learned the extent of Lyle's betrayal. He didn't know before with that reaction. I heard what he said. I heard his questions and they match what we heard here today. And," Violet said significantly, "the staff of the spa can corroborate that. They know he was in the massage room. They chased him out."

Fanny shuddered as Violet continued. "The only question left is how you got him to the garden?"

"Did you tell him you saw Fanny go out there?" Gervais demanded, sounding nearly gleeful. He was a mean version of Denny, Violet thought. Gervais leaned in aggressively. "That would have been easy enough. He was so angry about Fanny. Making something out of nothing is how Lyle described it when he told me about Michael wanting to leave the investments."

Pamela looked among her friends. She was searching for an ally *because* she believed Violet's lie. It was so easy to weave a plausible lie into a string of truths.

Violet guessed. "You could have simply followed him, but you didn't. Why would you? With the housekeeping key, you could get out of the lodge without going through the front doors. That would be an easy way to murder him and get back in."

Violet looked at Jack. He couldn't lay down the same lies Violet was about to without risking the investigation, so she carried on. "When the constables are finished searching your rooms, will they find the key, along with the things from our rooms, and of course Gervais's cuff links?"

Pamela gasped then, and any chance of keeping her lie faded when Fanny lunged for Pamela, but Michael caught his wife to stop her from reaching the pregnant woman. Fanny turned to words instead. "This is your fault! Michael thinks I...I...Michael..."

Michael rose slowly, gently pulling Fanny to him. "You framed me," he said to Pamela. "You framed me so well that Fanny thought I murdered my best friend. My brother."

"I didn't," Pamela cried.

"Your brother?" Gervais snorted and Violet shot him a look that demanded he close his mouth.

"You told me that you knew Lyle loved me," Fanny accused. "Pammy! You were the one who told me we needed to separate our families. To give us both peace.

You said that only I could make things right." Fanny was crying, tears mingling with the beads of sweat. "I would have been too afraid, but you told me it would be all right. You told me that things would be better. That Michael would understand."

"I didn't," Pamela said, shaking her head over and over again. "I didn't."

"Of course you did," Jovie said flatly. "I knew about that part. I even overheard part of it."

"You don't understand," Pamela moaned. "None of you understand what it's like except Jovie. No one wants you either, Jovie. Gervais will never actually love you. Not even your family wants you. But it's worse for me. Imagine it was your husband, and you were having his baby."

"But you aren't having his baby," Jovie told Pamela meanly, destroying that lie before it could take flight. "You lied to get Lyle to marry you. You did this to yourself, and then you did this to all of us." Jovie gestured to their friends. They were separated. No one except Michael and Fanny were together. They were, all of them, divided by the emotions of the last days. Vi doubted that there would be any recovery.

"You ruined us."

"We were already ruined," Pamela said hoarsely. "We were always going to be over. It was a long, slow death that started when *Lyle* wouldn't let his obsession with Fanny go. He only wanted her because she was Michael's. Just like everything between those two."

Ricky glanced among all of them. "That's not why you killed Lyle though, is it? We're stupid."

"What are you talking about?" Gervais asked lazily. "I'm certain I'm not stupid."

"Didn't Lyle's aunt just die?" Ricky lifted a brow and glanced meaningfully at Pamela. "The rich one?"

"Oh yes," Gervais cooed. "By Jove! We are stupid. He did inherit, didn't he?"

Michael nodded, staring at the other two. "It hasn't been transferred yet, but yes. It's his."

Gervais rubbed his hands together with out and out delight. "You're his heir, Pammy love. It was enough money that you didn't need him anymore, wasn't it? Or had he started to question how soon the baby was coming as compared to that party when you pulled him to bed? Had even your dulcet lies started to fail?"

"Money," Violet said. "Love gone wrong. Betrayal. All the classic motives. Go on, Pamela. Take this chance to say goodbye and maybe beg one of them to take your baby. The poor mite will be born in jail as it is."

"It's not fair," Pamela said, lips trembling. She'd gone from calculating to white and there was a protective hand on her stomach. She might not love anyone, Violet thought, but Pamela did—in fact—love that baby. If she hadn't believed Violet's lie, however, Pamela would never have asked for help. She did, however, believe, and it seemed she loved her baby enough to save it from the fate that Violet had laid out.

Pamela searched among them and then said, "Fanny?"

"Tell us the truth."

"Please, Fanny. Please save my baby."

"The truth," Fanny said evenly. Her arms were crossed over her chest like a schoolmarm. "I need to hear it."

Pamela slumped in despair. "It took too long to get

Lyle to make love to me and I got pregnant. It took so long to get his attention. I was too far along by then and thought I could lie. But he was starting to get suspicious. He'd have divorced me. I'd have been ruined and had a baby. Who would help me?"

"So you killed him," Fanny said flatly. All the tears had finally stopped, and Violet would have congratulated Fanny, but they still needed the confession.

"I tried to lie and say that babies came early in my family. He didn't believe me."

"So you killed him," Fanny repeated.

"I..."

"You're caught. You were seen. None of us killed him. None of us knew there was a reason to until after you were rifling through people's drawers."

"I didn't," Pamela wailed. "I didn't."

"You set my husband up as the killer, and now you're asking me to take your baby?" Fanny stepped away from Michael and leaned into Pamela's space, yanking her hand from her belly. "Tell the truth."

The roles had changed, and Fanny was the cruel emotionless one and Pamela was the weeping one.

"I told him you were in the garden. I said you were arguing with Michael, and you were probably looking for a shoulder to cry on. I was sarcastic and mean, but Lyle saw his chance. He left in moments. He barely looked at me as he put on his jacket. I had the key, I knew where he was going, I had told him where I'd seen you after all. I ran ahead and followed him to the garden, picked up a branch I had found earlier in the day when he had *left me alone, yet again.*"

"All of it," Fanny demanded.

"He was calling for you. I threw a rock so he turned, and then I hit him as hard as I could. I hit him for every time that he left me for you or compared me to you. I hit him for making me feel like nothing, and then I hit him again because I hated him. I had loved him and loved him and loved him, and he refused to love me back."

There it was. Jovie covered her face with her hands. Ricky lifted his brow again, sipped his cocktails and then rose slowly as though the show had ended.

"Bloody hell," Gervais muttered. "Bloody hell indeed."

"Take my baby?" Pamela begged Fanny who looked as surprised by Pamela's confession as Pamela herself seemed to be.

"No," Fanny said flatly and then she left the room, pausing in the doorway to say, "Come Michael."

He followed silently, without looking back at Pamela.

"Fanny!" Pamela cried. "Fanny! Please. Think of the baby."

Gervais snorted and followed after. Ricky and Jovie left next and then Lila and Denny. Violet glanced at Jack. He gave the barest nod.

"I'll make sure your baby is all right," Violet told Pamela.

Pamela's mouth was trembling as she nodded. A moment later Hamilton arrested her.

VIOLET OPENED ALL the windows before they left the room. She looked at Jack who looked back at her. "Did you want to go for a swim?"

He nodded, and they both changed in moments.

"I thought night swims would be ruined for us."

"But swimming didn't have anything to do with what happened, and we can't let killers take all of the joy out of our lives because the things we love were somehow associated with their crimes."

Violet didn't bother to reply as she dove into the water. It cooled her considerably and she gasped against the sudden chill. She was both morose and triumphant.

"I need to hold Vi and Agatha," Violet told Jack. "I want to go to whichever home has Victor and Kate nearby. I want to drink ginger wine, write stories with my brother, see the girls, check on Isolde. I want to send something to brighten the wart's day, and I want to tell my father I am never going anywhere he recommends again."

Jack laughed as he treaded water near Violet. Slowly, he reached out and snaked a hand around Violet's waist, pulling her close to him. "I have everything I want right here."

CHAPTER 18

"Gervais has a sister who hasn't been able to have a child," Jovie told Violet the next morning, tossing those wild curls.

Jovie looked sleepless and worried even though they'd discovered the killer. Or really, the killer had been pressured into confession. Violet was certain it wouldn't have worked if Pamela wasn't worried for her baby. It didn't surprise Violet to discover that the means to the end—the baby—had become more important than anything else until Pamela realized what would happen to her baby in the coming months.

"You think the sister will adopt the baby?"

Jovie nodded, rubbing the back of her neck. "I'm going to visit her, but a baby that is very likely her brother's baby? I think so. I'll tell her what I know and send her to you. I'm already sure she'll leap at the chance to adopt a niece or nephew and save them from an orphanage."

Violet would do anything—anything at all—for

Victor's daughters Agatha and little Vi. She had little doubt that she'd feel the same for her sister Isolde's baby who was due to arrive any day.

Violet nodded and then glanced at Jack. He was standing at the end of the oversized, wrap-around porch, smoking his cigar. There was nothing in his expression that said he was upset, but she knew he was upset all the same. Perhaps it was the slight downturn to his shoulders. Perhaps it was the twist to his mouth. Or the way his gaze reverted to her time and again, but Violet knew that he, like she, hated that they'd contributed to the arrest of a pregnant woman.

Guilty or not, they would be haunted by the idea of her baby being born in a prison. Pamela had been taken to the local police station the previous night and they'd all slept easier knowing the murderer was gone. To an extent, they were not worried about being attacked as they had been before they knew who the killer was, but the baby. The baby haunted all of them.

Hamilton had left early to write reports and would be back soon. He was doing what was necessary to ensure they'd be able to help the little one from the moment of his or her birth. The rest of Violet's party were only waiting for Ham's return before they took an auto back to London.

"Come with us," Violet told Jovie. "You don't have to be alone."

"It doesn't feel so," Jovie said. "Fanny broke with me. She told me that I should have trusted her. Michael told me that I should have told him what I knew. That I should have never let things get so bad for Fanny. He said it was my fault for not doing my family duty and speaking up."

Violet muttered a curse and then snapped her mouth shut. Blaming Jovie was the natural response for the self-absorbed. What about for Michael? What was his responsibility that he was so out of touch with his wife? Had his wife lost the ability to speak? Why was Jovie the one who had to have fixed it when she wasn't even a direct party in that relationship?

The problem was bigger than Michael and Fanny breaking with Jovie and revealing the level of their friendship. Jovie was beholden to Michael's parents as they had control of whatever her own parents had left her given they'd begrudgingly raised poor Jovie.

"Did you want me to have my man of business see if he can retrieve the money your parents left you?"

Jovie's gaze widened and her normally half-wicked expression faded into an emotional pleading. "You would do that?"

Violet nodded easily. Of course she would. She'd have helped Jovie even if she didn't like her. "Friends look after each other."

"Like I should have looked after Fanny," Jovie said, bowing her head.

"No," Violet disagreed. "No, not like that. Michael is blaming you for what he should have seen. It's easier to make you responsible than admit the fault might lie at his own feet."

"Thank you for looking after me and helping me," Jovie said. "All I wanted was to avoid Gervais. I never expected things to go this far."

Violet didn't bother to reiterate that if Michael had been looking after Jovie as he expected her to look after

Fanny, it wouldn't have been necessary for Jovie to attach herself to Violet's friends.

"Just come to London after you talk to Gervais's sister. I'll have my man see what he can do for you. If anything can be done, he can do it. If not we'll figure something out for you."

Jovie nodded and kissed Vi's cheek. Jovie went back inside the oversized lodge and Violet made her way to Jack. She wrapped her arms around his waist. "You smell nice."

He kissed the top of her head as he wrapped his arms around her as well. "I love you, Violet Wakefield."

"I love you," she echoed.

"You slept last night."

"I suppose that it felt as though we had won. We caught the killer, we found out *why,* and we agreed to help the baby and the brewer. I don't love what happened, but I do feel good about having done what we could."

"That we did." Jack pressed another kiss on her head and then tilted her face towards him. He placed a gentle kiss on her temple. On her nose. On each eye and then finally on her lips. "We did what we could. I just wish we could have stopped what happened instead."

They took a wide rocking chair near the edge of the large porch and watched the trees wave in the wind until the auto from the police stopped in front of the lodge. Hamilton got slowly out of the auto and walked up the steps. Jack called to Ham and he crossed to them. Jack handed over his cigar as Hamilton sighed and sat down.

"I hate cases like this," Ham said. "She wanted me to promise her that you could be counted on to help her baby. I swore you could."

"You know that I will," Violet replied. "We've already got an idea working, but I'll raise that baby myself before I see anything other than a good situation."

"I'll have the local boys tell her again. I know she's a killer, but I'd like to see her get updates on the child. At least until the baby is placed into a loving home." Ham puffed on the cigar and closed his eyes in the peace of the moment. Long minutes later, Lila and Denny joined them. None of them were joyous, but it helped being together.

"I gotta say," Denny said idly. "I love you all."

Violet smiled against Jack's shoulder. "I was just thinking the same thing."

"You would love my baby for me," Lila told Violet. It wasn't even a question, just a commentary on those other friends. "If I did something terrible, you would look after her. I wouldn't even have to ask."

"I would," Violet answered. Of course she would.

"You wouldn't place her somewhere else. You'd take her home with you. Love her like you'd love your own children. Raise her and look after her and settle her into life as well as possible. Without my even asking."

Violet nodded and she could feel Jack nodding as well. "Of course we would," Jack promised.

"That's why we want you to be her godparents."

Violet gasped, her eyes immediately welling with tears.

"This is where you say yes," Lila told Violet, handing over the handkerchief that had been at the ready. Lila knew Violet too well.

"Yes!"

"Of course," Jack echoed.

"We'll all look after your child," Hamilton told Lila and Denny. "Official godparents or not. However, we'll also

145

look after you, so we'll just be helping rather than taking over for you. What happens to you or me or any of us won't be what happened to Jovie's friends."

"Speaking of families," Lila began. Her voice was gentle and entirely not lazy. "Are you done fighting yours?"

"Yes," Ham agreed. "Violet is going to write to Rita, but —" He pulled a letter out of his pocket and handed it over to Violet. "Maybe you would send this with yours."

"I will," Violet promised. She curled her fingers against the desire to run inside, rip the letter open, and read it frantically.

"Tell her how pathetic he is," Lila demanded. "Say he cried."

"Tell her we miss her," Denny added. "Also our tables are out of balance without her, so we're going to need her to come back sooner or later. She can, however, leave Martha behind."

"That will definitely bring her home," Jack agreed. "Who wouldn't drop an overseas adventure seeing lands that few in England visit to come back and balance out a table?"

"Tell her I love her," Ham ended. His face was a furious flush under his beard, and his gaze was fixed on the trees beyond the lodge. Violet didn't even bother to hide her wide, delighted grin.

Denny cleared his throat and glanced at Lila. "That might do it."

"I would guess so," Lila said, laying her head against Denny's shoulder. "It would work for me."

Ham didn't look convinced, but Violet thought it would work as well. It might take Rita a little time; Violet had little doubt that Rita had been hurt by Hamilton. But an I'm sorry, I love you, I was wrong could go pretty far for many a woman.

"Ham," Violet told him, "even if she does come home..."

Vi waited until Ham's gaze met hers and then she glanced up at Jack and lifted a brow.

"It doesn't mean you don't have to beg," Jack told Ham seriously. "Bended knee, protestations of love, poetry and song. Rita isn't like Fanny. Rita is the captain of her own fate, the protagonist of her own story, the maker of her own dreams."

"Chocolate." Denny lifted Lila's hand and kissed her fingers.

"Dancing," Lila added.

"Just love Rita," Violet told Ham. "Just love her. Show her. Tell her. But love her."

"I already do."

The END

HULLO, my friends, I have so much gratitude for you reading my books. Almost as wonderful as giving me a chance are reviews, and indie folks, like myself, need them desperately! If you wouldn't mind, I would be so grateful for a review.

IF YOU WANT BOOK UPDATES, you could follow me on Facebook. Also, the sequel to this book is now available.

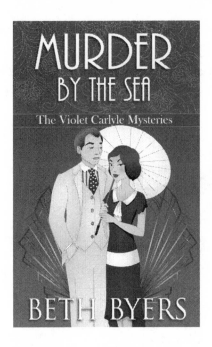

September 1925.

Vi and Jack have fled for the sea shore. Both to enjoy the sea air and to gather up their friend, Rita Russell who's come home at last. A little sea air, a ramble or two, afternoon naps, lingering mornings over a cup of Turkish coffee and perhaps all will be aright again.

Only one morning adventure ends with a body and yet again, Violet, Jack and their friends find themselves involved in a mysterious death. Will they be able to find the killer before he strikes again?

Order your copy here.

IF YOU ENJOY mysteries with a historical twist, scroll to the end for a sample of my new mystery series, The Hettie and Ro Adventures. The first book, Philanderers Gone is currently available.

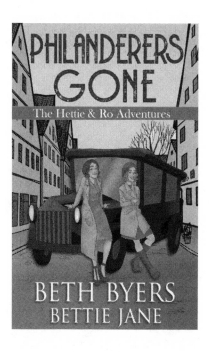

July 1922

If there's one thing to draw you together, it's shared misery.

Hettie and Ro married manipulative, lying, money-grubbing pigs. Therefore, they were instant friends. When those philandering dirtbags died, they found themselves the subjects of a murder investigation. Did they kill their husbands? No. Did they joke about it? Maybe. Do they need to find the killer before the crime is pinned on them? They do!

Join Hettie and Ro and their growing friendship as they delve into their own lives to find a killer, a best friend, and perhaps a brighter new outlook.

Order your copy here.

You may also enjoy my new historical paranormal 1920s series, The Bright Young Witches. The first book will be available soon.

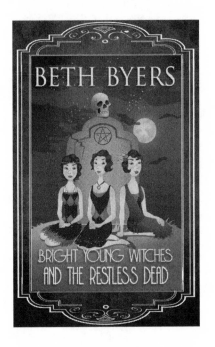

April 1922

When the Klu Klux Klan appears at the door of the Wode sisters, they decide it's time to visit the ancestral home in England.

With squabbling between the sisters, it takes them too long to realize that their new friend is being haunted. Now they'll have to set aside their fight, discover just why their friend is being haunted, and what they're going to do about it. Will they rid their friend of the ghost and out themselves as witches? Or will they look away?

Join the Wode as they rise up and embrace just who and what they are in this newest historical mystery adventure.

Order your copy here.

PHILANDERERS GONE PREVIEW

CHAPTER ONE

*T*he house was one of those ancient stone artisan-crafted monstrosities that silently, if garishly, announced buckets of bullion, ready money, the green, call it what you would, these folks were simply rolling in the good life. The windows were stained glass with roses and stars. The floor of wide-planked dark wood was probably Egyptian wood carried by camels and horses through deserts to the house. The furnishings were as finely dressed as the people gathered in celebration.

Hettie hid a smirk when a tall, beautiful, uniformed man slid through the crowd and leaned down, holding a tray of champagne and cocktails in front of her with a lascivious gaze. She wasn't quite sure if he appreciated the irony of his status as human art for the party, or if he embraced it and the opportunity it gave him to romance bored wives.

She was, very much, a bored wife. Or maybe disillu-sioned was the proper word. She took yet another flute of champagne and curled into the chair, pulling up her legs, leaving her shoes behind, and tucking her feet under her.

The sight of her husband laughing uproariously with a drink in each hand made her want to skip over to him and toss her champagne into his face. He had been drinking and partying so heavily, he'd become yellowed. The dark circles under his eyes emphasized his utter depravity. Or, then again, perhaps that was the disillusionment once again. Which came first? The depravity or the dark circles?

"Fiendish brute," Hettie muttered, lifting her glass at her own personal animal. Her husband, Harvey, wrapped his arm around another bloke, laughing into his face so raucously the poor man must have felt as though he'd stepped into a summer rain storm reeking of booze.

"Indeed," a woman said, and Hettie flinched, biting back a gasp to twist and see who had overheard her.

What a shocker! If Hettie had realized that anyone was around instead of swimming in that drunken sea of flesh, she'd have insulted him non-verbally. It was quite satisfying to speak her feelings out loud. Heaven knew he deserved every ounce of criticism.

She had nothing against fun. She had nothing against dancing, jazz, cocktails, or adventure. She did, however, have quite a lot against Harvey.

He had discovered her in Quebec City. Or rather he'd discovered she was an heiress and then pretended to discover her. He'd written her love letters and poems praising her green eyes, her red hair, and her pale skin as though being nearly dead-girl white were something to be envied. He'd made her feel beautiful even though she tended towards the plump, and he'd seemed oblivious to the spots she'd been dealing with on her chin and jaw line through all of those months.

A fraud in more ways than Hettie could count, he'd spent months prostrating himself at her feet, romancing her, wearing down her defenses until she'd strapped on the old white dress and discovered she'd gotten a drunken, spoiled, rude, lying ball and chain.

"Do you hate him too?" Hettie asked, wondering if she were commiserating with one of her husband's lovers. She would hardly be surprised.

"Oh, so much," the woman said. Her gaze met Hettie's and then they snorted almost in unison. "Such a wart. Makes everything a misery. It's a wonder that someone has not clocked him over the back of the head yet."

Hettie shocked herself with a laugh, totally unprepared to adore one of her husband's mistresses. "Oh! If only!" She lifted her glass in toast to the woman who grinned and lifted her own in return. "Cheers, darling."

"So, are you one of his lovers?" the woman asked.

"Wife," Hettie said, and the woman's gaze widened.

"Wife? I hardly think so."

"Oh, believe me," Hettie replied. "I wish it wasn't so."

"As his wife," the woman said with a frown, "I fear I must dispute your claim."

Hettie's gaze narrowed and she glanced back at Harvey. His blonde hair had been pomaded back, but some hijinks had caused the seal on the pomade to shift and it was flopping about in greasy hanks. He and the man he'd been molesting earlier clinked their glasses together and guzzled the cocktails. Harvey leaned into the man, and they both laughed raucously.

"Idiot," the woman said scornfully. "Look at him

gulping down a drink that anyone with taste would have sipped. The blonde one, he must be yours?"

Hettie nodded with disgust and grimaced. "Unfortunately, yes, the blond wart with the pomade gone wrong is my ball and chain. So the other fool is yours?"

The woman laughed. "I suppose I sounded almost jealous. I wasn't, you know. I'd have been happy if Leonard was yours."

"Alas, my fate has been saddled with yon blond horse, Harvey."

They grinned at each other and then the other woman held out her hand. "Ro Lavender. So pleased to meet someone with my same ill-fate. Makes me feel less alone."

Hettie held out her own hand. "Hettie Hughes. I thought Leonard's last name was Ripley."

"Oh, it is," Ro said. "I try not to tie myself to his wagon unless it benefits me. At the bank, for instance."

"Shall we be bosom friends?" Hettie asked.

"I just read that book. Do you love it as well?"

"I'm Canadian," Hettie replied, standing to twine her arm through Ro's. "Of course I've read it. Anne, Green Gables, Diana, Gilbert, Marilla, and Prince Edward Island were fed to me with milk as a babe. Only those of us with a fiendish brute for a husband can truly understand the agony of another. How did you get caught?"

"Family pressure. We were raised together. Quite close friends over the holidays, but I never knew the real him until after."

Hettie winced. "Love letters for me," she said disgustedly. "You'd think modern women such as ourselves wouldn't have been quite so..."

"Stupid," Ro replied, tucking her bobbed hair behind her ear.

The laughter from the crowd around the table became too much to hear anything and Hettie asked, "Shall we escape into the nighttime?"

"Let's go to Prince Edward Island," Ro joked. "Is it magical there? I've always wanted to go."

"I've never been," Hettie admitted, "but I have a sudden desperate need. Let's flee in the darkness. You know they won't miss us until their fathers insist they arrive somewhere with their respectable wives on their arms."

"Or, I could murder yours and you could murder mine, and we could create our freedom. If our families want respectable, I would definitely respect a woman that could rid herself of these monsters."

"That sounds lovely. Until we can plan our permanent freedom, I suppose our best option is simply to retreat."

Ro lifted her glass in salute and sipped.

Hettie set aside her champagne flute and then turned to face her husband, who had pulled Mrs. Stone, the obvious trollop, into his lap and was kissing her extravagantly. Hettie scrunched up her nose and gagged a little. Mrs. Stone had been in Nathan Brighton's lap just last week.

"She slept with Leonard too," Ro informed Hettie in an even tone.

Hettie reveled in the camaraderie she found in Ro's resigned tone. "Have you met Mr. Stone?"

Ro nodded. "He doesn't realize. He's not the type of man to be cuckolded like this. So...overtly. Have you heard of the marriage act they've proposed?"

Hettie nodded with little doubt that her eyes had

brightened like that of a child at Christmas. "I will be there on the very first day. If Harvey had any idea, any at all, he'd be rolling over in his future grave. The money's mine, you know? My aunt never liked Harvey and she tied up my money tightly. He gets what he wants because it's easier to give it to him than listen to him whine, but he won't get a half-penny from me the day I can file divorce papers. They say it's going to go through."

"I couldn't care less about the money," Ro replied. "Though my money is coming from a still-living aunt. Leonard has enough, I suppose, but his eye is definitely on Aunt Bette's fortune."

"So he needs to go before she does."

Ro choked on her laughter so hard she had to wipe away tears.

"Darling!" Harvey hollered across the room. "We're going down to Leonard's yacht. You can get yourself home, can't you?"

Hettie closed her eyes for a moment before she replied. "Of course I can. Don't fall in." She crossed her fingers so only Ro could see. Ro's laugh made Hettie grin at Harvey. He gave her a bit of a confused look. Certainly he had shouted his exit with the hope she wouldn't scold him. Foolish man! She'd welcome him moving into Mrs. Stone's bed permanently and leaving Hettie behind.

The handsome servant from earlier picked up Hettie's abandoned glass and shot her a telling, not quite disapproving look.

"Oh-ho," Hettie said, making sure the man heard her. "We've been overheard."

"We've been eavesdropped," Ro agreed. Then with a lifted brow to the human work of art serving champagne,

"Boyo, our husbands are aware of our lack of love. There's no chance for blackmail here."

"Does your aunt feel the same?" he asked insinuatingly.

Hettie stiffened, but Ro only laughed. "Do you think she hasn't heard the tale of that lush Leonard? She's written me stiff-upper-lip letters. 'Watch your step and your mouth or you'll lose your position despite your pretty face,'" she repeated in a pinched tone. "'It doesn't matter how you feel, only how you look. No one is paying you to think.'"

The servant flushed and bowed deeply, shooting them both a furious expression as he silently backed away.

"Cheeky lad," Hettie muttered. "You scolded him furiously. Are you sure you weren't taking out your rage on the poor fellow?"

"Cheeky, yes," Ro agreed. She placed a finger on her lip as she considered Hettie's question and then agreed. "Too harsh as well. I suppose I would need to apologize if he didn't threaten to blackmail me."

"But pretty," they said nearly in unison. They laughed as the servant overhead them and gave them both a sultry glance.

"Oh no, boyo," Ro told him. "Toddle off now, darling. We've had quite our fill of philandering, reckless men. You've missed your window." Ro's head cocked as she glanced Hettie over. "Well, shall we?"

"Shall we what, love?"

Ro grinned wickedly. "Shall we be bosom friends? Soul sisters after one shared breath?"

"Let's. As the man I thought was my soulmate was an utter disaster, I'll take a soul sister as a replacement."

They sent a servant to get an auto. "I was thinking of

going to a bottle party later," Ro told her. "At a bath house. That just might distract us."

Hettie tilted her head as she considered. "Harvey does expect me to go home."

Ro lifted her brows and waited.

"So we must, of course, disillusion him as perfectly as he has me."

"There we go!" Ro cheered, shaking her hands over head. "It is only fair. I have been considering a trip to the Paris fashion salons."

"Yes," Hettie immediately agreed, knowing it would enrage Harvey, who preferred her tucked away in case he needed her. "We should linger in Paris then swing over to Spain."

"Oooh, Spain!"

"Italy," Hettie suggested just to see if Ro would agree.

"Yes!"

"Russia?"

Ro paused. "Perhaps Cote d'Azure? Egypt? Somewhere warmer. I always think of snow when I think of Russia, and I only like it with cocoa and sleigh rides. Perhaps one or two days a year."

"Agreed—" Hettie trailed off, eyes wide, as she watched Mrs. Stone enthusiastically kiss the cheeky servant from earlier and then adjust her coat. She winked at Hettie on the way out, caring little that both of them knew Mrs. Stone would be climbing into Harvey's bed later. Or perhaps it was Harvey who would be climbing into Mr. Stone's bed. "Is her husband really blind to it?"

"Oh yes." Ro laughed. "He's quite a bit older, you know, and even more old-fashioned than my grandfather. He's Victorian through and through. He probably has a codicil in the will about her remarrying. The type of thing that cuts her off if she doesn't remain true to him. Especially since he's in his seventies, and she's thirty? Perhaps?"

Hettie shook her head and put Mrs. Stone from her mind. "They have a rather outstanding blackberry wine here. Shall we just—ah—borrow a bottle or two for the party?"

Ro nodded and walked across to the bar, digging through the bottles to pull out a full bottle of blackberry wine, another of gin, and a third of a citrus liqueur. "Hopefully someone will think to bring good mixers." She handed one of the bottles to Hettie and then tucked one under each arm.

The butler eyed them askance when they asked for their coats as a black cab arrived in front.

"Don't worry, luv," Ro told the butler. "Your master doesn't mind."

None of them believed that whopper of a lie, but Ro's cheerful proclamation somehow made it acceptable.

"Thief," Hettie hissed innocently as the driver opened the door to the black cab. She dove inside. Struggling with the cork, she asked, "Are we going to the baths nude or shall we grab bathing costumes?"

"My brother-in-law lives with us," Ro said, looking disgusted. "I'll be going nude before I go back and face that one. Oh…" Her head cocked as the black cab sped up. "I think that's him!"

"I'm a bit too round to really want to go full starkers," Hettie said, uninterested in seeing the brother-in-law.

"The men love the curves," Ro told her. "If you wanted to step out on your Harvey, you'd just need to up the attitude and cast a come-hither gaze."

"Like this?" Hettie asked, attempting one but feeling as though she must look as though she had something in her eye.

"Like this," Ro countered, glancing at Hettie out of the corner of her eye. "I'm thinking of a scrumptious plate of biscuits."

Hettie tried it and Ro bit back a laugh. "Are you angry with the biscuits?"

"Let me try imagining cakes. I do prefer a lemon cake." Hettie glanced at Ro out of the corner of her eye, imagining a heavily-iced lemon cake, and then smiled just a little.

"No, no," Ro said, showing Hettie again what to do.

"Oh! I know." Hettie imagined the divorce act that the parliament was considering.

"Yes! Now you've got it! Was it a box of chocolates?"

Hettie confessed, sending Ro into a bout of laughter and tears that saw them all the way to Hettie's hotel. From her hotel room to Ro's rooms, there were random burst of giggles and stray tears. Once they reached to bath house, Ro said, "I'll be drinking to that divorce act tonight. Possibly for the rest of my life."

"If it frees me," Hettie told Ro dryly, "I'd paper my house with copies of it to celebrate those who saved us from a fate I should have known better than to fall into."

Order your copy here.

co-written with Bettie Jane

Philanderers Gone

Adventurer Gone

Holiday Gone

Aeronaut Gone

Prankster Gone

The Poison Ink Mysteries

Death By the Book

Death Witnessed

Death by Blackmail

Death Misconstrued

Deathly Ever After

Death in the Mirror

A Merry Little Death

The 2nd Chance Diner Mysteries

Spaghetti, Meatballs, & Murder

Cookies & Catastrophe

Poison & Pie

Double Mocha Murder

Cinnamon Rolls & Cyanide

Tea & Temptation

Donuts & Danger

Scones & Scandal

Lemonade & Loathing

Wedding Cake & Woe

Honeymoons & Honeydew

The Pumpkin Problem

ALSO BY AMANDA A. ALLEN

The Mystic Cove Mommy Mysteries

Bedtimes & Broomsticks

Runes & Roller Skates

Banshees and Babysitters

Hobgoblins and Homework

Christmas and Curses

Valentines & Valkyries

The Rue Hallow Mysteries

Hallow Graves

Hungry Graves

Lonely Graves

Sisters and Graves

Yule Graves

Fated Graves

Ruby Graves

The Inept Witches Mysteries

(co-written with Auburn Seal)

Inconvenient Murder

Moonlight Murder

Bewitched Murder